Emma Ansky-Levine
and Her Mitzvah Machine

LAWRENCE BUSH

Emma Ansky-Levine
AND HER
Mitzvah Machine

Illustrated by
JOEL ISKOWITZ

UAHC Press • New York, New York

Library of Congress Cataloging-in-Publication Data

Bush, Lawrence.
    Emma Ansky-Levine and her mitzvah machine / Lawrence Bush;
illustrated by Joel Iskowitz.
       p.   cm.
    Includes bibliographical references.
    Summary: For her twelfth birthday, Emma receives a special Mitzvah
Machine, which helps her discover her Jewish identity and the true
meaning of becoming a Bat Mitzvah.
    ISBN 0–8074–0458–6 : $7.95
    [1. Bat mitzvah—Fiction. 2. Jews—Fiction.] I. Iskowitz, Joel,
ill. II. Title.
PZ7.B9654Em   1991
[Fic]—dc20   90–24491
                                                          CIP
                                                          AC

THIS BOOK IS PRINTED ON RECYCLED PAPER

Copyright © 1991 by Lawrence Bush
Manufactured in the United States of America
10 9 8 7 6 5 4 3 2 1

For Rusty, my brother

Contents

1

The Mayor

Two strangers arrived on Emma Ansky-Levine's block during the week of her twelfth birthday, September 10. The first was a homeless man with two torn, overstuffed plastic shopping bags. He appeared one sunny morning on the bench at the foot of the grassy hill where Emma usually walked Keppy the Enormous Dog. Huddled inside a dirty coat, he was muttering to himself through a straggly beard and turning his head as if he had friends listening on either side. Emma wondered what the conversation was all about, but she wasn't willing to get close enough to hear. There was a rotten smell in the air, and it was coming from his direction.

Keppy had a different idea about smells and began tugging Emma towards the bench. Emma yanked on the leash and cried, "Keppy! Heel!" Keppy knew her commands (fortunately for Emma, who weighed only seventy-eight pounds, twenty less than her dog) and led the way to the bald spot on the hilltop.

The stranger was still on the bench in the late afternoon, a sorry sight for all the grown-ups to see as they returned from work to the apartment buildings on either side of the hill. The next morning he remained, and on into the evening. Emma nicknamed him "The Mayor," for whenever she saw him his lips were moving, as if he were making a speech.

1

She felt uneasy about using the nickname in front of others; Emma didn't want them to think she was a tease. She soon realized, however, that most of her neighbors used even worse names for the man: bum, tramp, psycho, drunkard, derelict, lowlife. Throughout the week, Emma heard them complaining about him in the hallways, elevator, and laundry room.

"Have you seen that bum? Someone ought to call the police. It must be against the law to smell like that!"

"It's disgusting! Why doesn't he get a job! It's not as if he's handicapped or anything."

Then they would notice Emma and say something friendly to her. They seemed to have two faces, and Emma wasn't sure which was real. She meant to ask her parents about some of the things she overheard. Were homeless people always crazy, lazy, or drunk? Was it true that a lot of them had huge stashes of money hidden away? What would he do when the winter snows fell? But she kept forgetting to ask; by the time Emma would return from her walks with Keppy to her apartment on the tenth floor, the Mayor would be out of sight, out of mind, returning to her memory only at strange times, like in the shower, or while she drifted off to sleep.

The second stranger arrived in a heavy carton that was delivered to the Ansky-Levine apartment on the morning of Emma's birthday. "It's from Jerusalem," announced her father, Bruce Levine, looking at the postmark on the package as the delivery man wheeled it in on a hand truck. "It must be from my crazy uncle in Israel."

"You mean, Uncle Izzy?" Emma threw her arms around Keppy, whose head was as big as a basketball. "He's the one who gave you your name!" Keppy's name meant "head" in Yiddish. "She's only a puppy now," Izzy had said on that day, six years ago, when Emma had brought her home from the ASPCA, "but look at the size of her head! And those

paws! This little brown mutt will someday be known as Keppy the Enormous Dog!"

Emma remembered Uncle Izzy as a fast-talking, skinny old guy with a short gray beard that made his bald head look almost upside-down. In fact, whenever Emma's father spoke of Uncle Izzy he would say, "He's got his head screwed on backwards," for Izzy had a reputation as an inventor of strange and useless machines.

Emma read out loud a note that was stapled to the carton beneath its brown wrapping.

> *Dear Emma: I can't be with you for your birthday this year, but I do promise to be there for your bat mitzvah next year.*

"Am I going to have a bat mitzvah next year?" she asked her mother, Sharon Ansky.

"That's up to you, sweetheart. I don't know if a year is enough time to get ready." Sharon looked at Bruce, who shrugged.

"All I remember about Hebrew school," he said, "is that I always wanted to be somewhere else."

"Well, I didn't even get to *go*," Sharon said. "Girls weren't taken seriously back then." She turned back to Emma. "We could ask to enroll you at the synagogue, but you'd have to take it as seriously as we take *you*."

Emma frowned and read on:

> *Meanwhile, I'm sending you my Mitzvah Machine—the only one of its kind in the world!*

"What's a Mitzvah Machine?"

"God only knows!" said her father.

"Well, what's a mitzvah?"

"It's a religious kind of thing," he tried to explain. "A Jewish good deed."

A good deed. Suddenly Emma remembered all the questions she had meant to ask about the Mayor. "How about—"

"Look," her father interrupted, plucking Uncle Izzy's note from Emma's hand, "let's finish reading so we can see what kind of junk is in the box, okay? And don't be disappointed, Em—you'll get plenty of other presents at your party today."

Emma began to daydream about gifts while her father read:

> *Your father will call the Mitzvah Machine a piece of junk. But wasn't he also the one who said that Keppy would be a pest?*

Keppy's tail went *thump! thump!* at the sound of her name. Emma peeked at her father, then giggled. He read on:

> *So plug in the Mitzvah Machine and say goodbye to ever being bored. Happy birthday!*
>
> > B'Shalom,
> > Uncle Izzy

The Mitzvah Machine looked like a computer monitor shaped like the tablets of the Ten Commandments. "Let's hope this thing doesn't blow every fuse in the building," Bruce grumbled as he bent to plug it in.

The monitor instantly lit. Words appeared:

SHALOM, EMMA. HAPPY BIRTHDAY!

"What'm I supposed to do?" Emma shrieked as her dad began to tear through the packing box to find instructions.

HOW'S KEPPY?

"How does it know our names?"

"Obviously," Sharon said, "Uncle Izzy must've programmed it to say certain things."

Bruce was up to his ankles in paper and cardboard. "There's nothing else, not even a keyboard. I guess the disk drive is built right into the machine and has just one program, like a video game."

```
I WANT TO GIVE YOU
YOUR FIRST LESSON.
```

"Lesson?" Emma cried. "Fooey on youey! It's my birthday today!" She looked up at her father. "Too bad it's *not* a video game, huh?"

```
DO AS I SAY AND I GUARANTEE YOU
MORE FUN THAN YOU'VE EVER HAD WITH
A VIDEO GAME.
```

Emma's eyes grew wide. "Ma? Is this machine talking to me, or what?"

"Of course not." Sharon patted the Mitzvah Machine. "Hm? Are you reading my little girl's mind?" The screen went blank. "Come," Sharon said, "I need help getting ready for the party this afternoon. Let's turn it off for a while."

"There's no power switch," Emma observed.

"Pull the plug, then," her mother said impatiently.

Keppy had settled on the floor right in front of the electrical outlet. She growled when Bruce tried to nudge her aside with his foot. "Keppy!" Emma scolded her dog. "Be nice!"

"Leave it on, then!" Sharon insisted. "Let's get to work!"

"I wonder what happened to my lesson," Emma said.

The monitor lit up:

DO YOU WANT THAT LESSON OR NOT?

"No!" she shouted and ran, laughing, from the room.

"Make a wish and blow, Emma!"

Everyone was gathered around the dining room table, kids and adults, their eyes bright from the fun of singing "Happy Birthday" together. For a moment Emma wondered if she wasn't a bit old for this fuss, blowing out candles and making wishes, but then the little girl inside of her thought of a dozen wishes to make. *I wish Mom would let me cut my hair short . . . but then I wouldn't have the guts to do it, probably! . . . I wish I could get Excellent in math without taking any tests. . . . No, come on, think of something that really could happen. . . . I wish Richie Finestone's present to me is as nice as that bracelet he gave Deborah Schott the Snot. . . .*

"Blow before the candles melt!" her mother warned. So Emma blew before really settling on a wish. Everybody clapped hands, and then Bruce began to divide up the cake. There wasn't room enough for all of the guests to eat at the table, so the party spread throughout the apartment again. Emma carried her slice—chocolate with whipped cream, just as she had requested!—over to the living room window at which Keppy was sitting with her snout on the sill.

"Hi, big girl," Emma said in the high voice that she used only for Keppy, and which always got that shaggy tail to wag.

Not this time: Keppy looked anxiously at Emma, then turned her sad eyes back to the window.

"Aw, Keppy!" Emma cooed. "I thought you were having a good time at my party! Do you have to go out?"

Keppy whimpered.

"What is it? What's out there?" Emma looked and spotted

him: the Mayor, shuffling past the garbage cans at the back of their building and carrying a crumpled brown bag. *That's probably his lunch,* she realized—*somebody else's garbage! I forgot all about him! I made all those wishes without even thinking of him!*

"Yuch," said Emma's good friend Danny Rosen, pressing his nose against the window. "Look at that guy eating garbage."

"We have so much food in here," Emma said. "Half of it's going to end up in those cans."

"Isn't he lucky? Yum!" Danny smirked, rubbing his tubby belly.

Emma shoved his shoulder. "That's not what I mean and you know it! We ought to go give him something to eat right now."

"Are you crazy? That guy's diseased!"

"Danny, you're disgusting."

"*I'm* disgusting?"

"Come on!" she cried. "Nobody's doing anything to help him!"

Sharon was carrying a tray of cookies into the living room and saw her daughter in an argument. "What's going on, you two?"

"Emma's in love," Danny hooted.

Emma tried to ignore him. "Mom, I want to bring some food to the Mayor."

"The who?"

"The garbage man!" Danny yelped, scooting away to join the other kids, who were just starting to lay aside their cake plates and dance.

Emma's mother put down the cookie tray and touched Emma's shoulder—and then Emma began to cry. The tears came as a surprise even to her, but so had Danny's wisecracks, and so had her neighbors' heartless conversations. "Baby, what's the matter?" Sharon said. "What makes you so sensitive all of a sudden?"

"What makes everybody else so *creepy* all of a sudden?" Emma retorted through her tears. "They're all just as dirty and smelly as he is!"

"Who?" Sharon pleaded to know.

Emma pointed out the window. "We have all this food, while he . . ."

Her mother glanced out and saw the Mayor in the alley. "Oh, absolutely not! I know you want to be nice, but . . . we're in the middle of your birthday party! Emma, for all you know, that man is completely crazy!"

"For all *you* know," Emma replied, "he's Uncle Izzy!"

Sharon pressed her palm against her daughter's forehead. "Are you feeling sick?"

Emma batted away her mother's hand. "I'm sick of everyone here!" She ran to her room, with Keppy bounding after.

The Mitzvah Machine was blinking:

TZEDAKAH

"Stupid machine," Emma muttered, wiping her eyes. "Who needs a lesson now?" *What I need is a way to teach* them *all a lesson! They should all have to eat out of a garbage can for supper!* She curled up on the floor with her Enormous Dog. "Oh, Keppy, what if you ever get lost? You'll get all rumpled and stinky like the Mayor, and then what? They'll call the ASPCA and put you to sleep!"

Somebody knocked at her door. "Emma?" It was Danny Rosen. "I'm sorry, Em." He ducked his curly head into the room and spotted Uncle Izzy's invention. "Hey, neat! When'd you get the computer?"

"It's not a computer," she said, "it's a Mitzvah Machine. Anyway, none of your business. Why don't you go stuff your face until you turn into a hippo?"

"Hey, c'mon," he protested. "I said I'm sorry."

"Big deal." Emma hugged her dog even tighter.

Danny let his eyes stray back to the Mitzvah Machine. "How come it says 'Tzedakah'?" he said.

"What's a mitzvah?" she asked, still in an angry tone.

"I asked first!"

"So you answer first, too! What's a mitzvah? And don't act like I'm stupid!"

Danny crossed his eyes and let his tongue hang out. Emma laughed and let go of her snippy mood. She remembered her father's explanation: "Is it, like, a good deed?"

"Some of them are good deeds, yeah," Danny said. "Mitzvot are things you're supposed to do if you're Jewish, like . . . like, praying is a mitzvah, and lighting candles for Shabbat . . ." He pointed to the monitor. "That's a mitzvah—tzedakah."

"What does it mean?"

"It's when you give charity."

"Charity?" Emma stared at the Mitzvah Machine and sounded out the word: "Tze . . . tzedakah."

Suddenly the green monitor light increased in brightness and flared to yellow as if it were about to explode. Emma heard groans and sighs coming from the living room. She and Danny ran out to see what was happening.

The electrical power had died. The CD player, the coffee machine, the refrigerator, the clock—everything that needed electricity had stopped working at the same moment.

"Yahoo!" cried Danny. "A blackout!"

"They better fix it soon, or all the ice cream is going to melt!" moaned Sharon, standing at the refrigerator.

"It's the whole building," said Bill Trible, Bruce's best friend, who had been talking on the telephone with his elderly grandmother on the first floor when the power failed. "I've got to go help Grams."

Bruce took Emma aside as soon as he spotted her. "Pull out the plug on that damned computer!" he said in an angry whisper. "We're liable to get sued!"

Emma did as she was told; the monitor was blank now, anyway. Alone in her room, she giggled and bounced gaily on her bed, thinking, *Yay, Uncle Izzy!*

When she took Keppy for a walk at dusk, the blackout had not ended. Candles were lit in windows in both apartment buildings, reminding Emma of her birthday cake. By now, however, she had figured out what to wish for and how to make it come true.

The evening air was cool, and some people were putting food from their refrigerators onto their windowsills to prevent spoilage. They seemed mostly in a good mood, thanks to the excitement of the emergency. Neighbors who had lived in the same building for years without ever having a conversation were suddenly borrowing candles and flashlights and having long talks about the mysterious blackout. What could have caused it? Why had it affected only their buildings, instead of the whole block? Why was it taking the electric company so long to locate the problem? Were they going to have to dig up the street?

Emma and Keppy made an appearance at every first-floor window. Keppy was pulling Emma's old, squeaky red wagon, which was tied to the dog's collar by a long piece of twine. The wagon carried an assortment of candles and flashlight batteries that Emma had bought at the supermarket with her birthday money.

"Hello, Mrs. Franklin." Emma shone her flashlight into her own face. "It's me, yeah. Today was my twelfth birthday! . . . Thank you, it was a happy one. . . . Do you want to trade some of that Swiss cheese for a candle? It's probably going to get all gooey, anyway."

Knock knock. "Mr. Peretz? Open the window. . . . Hi. You need a candle? How about trading an apple for it?"

Most of her neighbors assumed Emma was feeding the food to Keppy—and once in a while she did give a scrap to the dog, to keep her happily at work pulling the wagon as it filled up. Only Bill's grandmother, Mrs. Trible, asked before making her contribution: "What are you going to do with a wagonful of food?"

Emma glanced nervously towards the bottom of the hill where, in the gathering darkness, she could barely make out the Mayor, huddled on his bench. If she told Mrs. Trible the truth, Mrs. Trible would tell Bill, and Bill would tell her parents . . .

"I'm doing a mitzvah, Mrs. Trible."

The old woman was sitting in her wheelchair by the window, peering down the hill. "What does that mean, dear?" The Tribles were not Jewish.

"It's something that makes you feel like you're an okay person," Emma said, "you know what I mean?"

"I'll say I do!" Mrs. Trible replied. "If I didn't think I was an 'okay person,' I wouldn't have bothered living to be ninety-two!"

Emma laughed. "Wow! Maybe just living that long is a mitzvah!"

Mrs. Trible held up a long, skinny finger. "Only if you do something worthwhile with your life." With a groan she stood and reached to the top of her refrigerator. "I'll give you a nice loaf of bread for your wagon, how's that? And I think I'll also give you . . ."—she shuffled to a drawer and took out a pair of brown leather gloves—"these. Mr. Trible used to wear them when he was alive, God bless him."

When Emma reached up to the window, Mrs. Trible patted her hand. "It's nice what you're doing, Emma. If we don't look out for one another, we'll all just disappear."

"Thanks, Mrs. Trible," Emma said in a small voice.

"Thank *you*, dear." Mrs. Trible sank back into her wheelchair with a sigh.

Now came the most difficult job: getting the food to the Mayor. Even from a hundred feet away, Emma could smell his awful stink. Maybe he *was* a real sicko, just as everyone said! And maybe if she came close he'd jump up and try to drag her off! She shuddered at the thought, then grasped Keppy by the collar, switched on her flashlight, and walked towards the bench with her wagon bouncing and squeaking behind.

He was sitting between his filthy shopping bags, as usual, mumbling to himself too quickly and quietly to be understood. Briefly Emma saw the glint of his eyes in her light, but then the Mayor buried his face in one of his bags. She turned off the beam at once. *He must think I'm the police or something!*

"Excuse me?" she called from a distance. "Sir?" *I wonder if anyone in the world knows his real name.* "There's lots of food here for you, if you're hungry . . ."

She could still hear him muttering as she untied Keppy from the wagon. "I'm leaving now," she said. "You can have the wagon. There are a couple of sharp spots where it's rusted . . . be careful, okay?"

I've probably just been talking to myself, Emma thought as she hurried away, up the hill.

Someone at the crest was shining a light into her face. "Em? That you?" It was Danny, a rotund shadow in the darkness.

"This blackout's so great," he said as she reached the hilltop. "Friday the thirteenth! We ought to run around spooking people."

Emma sat on the grass, with Keppy panting by her side. Danny began to sweep the beam from his flashlight across the hillside. "Hey, there's that guy! What's he got?"

"Turn off your light!" Emma snatched Danny's flashlight and clicked it off. "Let it be dark," she said in a gentler voice. "Maybe we'll see meteors."

"Neat." Danny looked skywards.

Emma, too, kept her eyes peeled skywards, her head against Keppy's rump, while she listened to the faint squeaking of the red wagon's wheels at the foot of the hill.

The sound faded beyond her earshot. "Tell me more about tzedakah," she said.

Just as she spoke that Hebrew word, the electric lights in both buildings blazed on. Cheers rose up from a dozen open windows. Emma bolted up and stared about her.

"Aw, nuts!" Danny groaned. "I wanted it to stay dark until midnight!"

The Mayor and the wagon were nowhere in sight. "Tzedakah," Emma whispered again, and held her breath, as if the word were a Jewish abracadabra.

"Mm, look at that moon," Danny said, pointing to a white crescent that was just beginning to rise over the roof of their apartment building.

Emma nodded slowly, and then smiled, and then almost giggled out loud. *I wonder if it's nighttime in Jerusalem, too,* she thought, waving at the moon and imagining her Uncle Izzy peering up to see the same thin strip of light.

2

The Red Scarf

"It's not because you're a girl!" Danny Rosen hollered at Emma Ansky-Levine as she plopped onto her bed with a frown on her face. "There are plenty of girls in my Hebrew school who become bat mitzvah! But you only have a year to go before you're thirteen."

"So what?" Emma said. "What do you have to do, go to college first?"

"You've got to know how to read Hebrew! You've got to know something about Judaism, about the Torah. No offense, Emma—you're smarter than me, maybe, but your family, boy—"

"Don't call me 'boy,' " Emma said.

"You guys don't act like you're Jewish at all," he said. "You've got a lot to learn if you want a real bat mitzvah!"

"Well," Emma said, "I've got that to help me." She pointed at her Mitzvah Machine.

"Yeah, right." Danny puffed out his chubby cheeks. "All that thing does is blow the electricity!"

Emma had not plugged in her Mitzvah Machine since the blackout, two weeks earlier. She felt nervous even about touching it, but Danny's sarcasm provoked her into action. She hopped off the bed and crouched by the outlet. The monitor, shaped like the tablets of the Ten Commandments, lit up.

Suddenly the bedroom door burst open. Both kids jumped

in fright. Keppy the Enormous Dog had come for a visit. "God, she scared me!" Danny confessed, running his fingers through his hair.

A red chiffon scarf was hanging from Keppy's slobbery jaws. "Drop it," Emma commanded. "Ooh, where did this come from?" She fetched the damp scarf and draped it across her narrow shoulders. "It's beautiful! Finders keepers!"

"In that case, it belongs to Keppy," Danny said, scratching the dog's huge head. "Maybe she'll trade it for a giant milk-bone."

Emma's smile sagged as she remembered: "Oh, I know— it's Vanessa Trible's. She came for dinner with Bill a few days ago. It looked great, braided in with that black hair of hers. Oh, darn." She held the scarf out to Danny. "Take it away."

"You don't want it?"

"Are you kidding?" Emma stuffed it into Danny's hand. "What would happen if she saw me wearing it?"

Danny shrugged. "I bet you she won't even miss it. Stick it in a drawer for a couple of months."

"Danny! They're my parents' best friends! I see them all the time!"

"Good. So maybe she'll let you keep it if you return it to her, you know, with a certain look on your face. . . ."

Emma glanced at the Mitzvah Machine's rippling field of green light. "I don't even like Vanessa Trible," she murmured. "She acts so stuck up sometimes, because she's an artist. . . . Sometimes I think my father's in love with her! He sure acts it, always complimenting her and stuff."

Danny dangled the scarf in front of her. "Keep it."

Emma clucked her tongue and turned towards the window.

The Mitzvah Machine began to hum. "Uh-oh," Danny said. "There goes the electricity!"

Hebrew words appeared on the monitor:

לֹא תִּגְנֹב:

"What is that?" Emma said suspiciously. Danny began to sound out the letters.

Still humming, Uncle Izzy's machine filled its screen with Hebrew:

אָנֹכִי יְהוָה אֱלֹהֶיךָ אֲשֶׁר הוֹצֵאתִיךָ מֵאֶרֶץ מִצְרַיִם
מִבֵּית עֲבָדִים: לֹא־יִהְיֶה לְךָ אֱלֹהִים אֲחֵרִים עַל־
פָּנָי: לֹא־תַעֲשֶׂה לְךָ פֶסֶל וְכָל־תְּמוּנָה אֲשֶׁר בַּשָּׁמַיִם
מִמַּעַל וַאֲשֶׁר בָּאָרֶץ מִתַּחַת וַאֲשֶׁר בַּמַּיִם מִתַּחַת
לָאָרֶץ: לֹא־תִשְׁתַּחֲוֶה לָהֶם וְלֹא תָעָבְדֵם כִּי אָנֹכִי
יְהוָה אֱלֹהֶיךָ אֵל קַנָּא פֹּקֵד עֲוֹן אָבֹת עַל־בָּנִים
עַל־שִׁלֵּשִׁים וְעַל־רִבֵּעִים לְשֹׂנְאָי: וְעֹשֶׂה חֶסֶד לַאֲלָפִים
לְאֹהֲבַי וּלְשֹׁמְרֵי מִצְוֹתָי: ס לֹא תִשָּׂא אֶת־שֵׁם־
יְהוָה אֱלֹהֶיךָ לַשָּׁוְא כִּי לֹא יְנַקֶּה יְהוָה אֵת אֲשֶׁר־
יִשָּׂא אֶת־שְׁמוֹ לַשָּׁוְא: פ
זָכוֹר אֶת־יוֹם הַשַּׁבָּת לְקַדְּשׁוֹ: שֵׁשֶׁת יָמִים תַּעֲבֹד
וְעָשִׂיתָ כָּל־מְלַאכְתֶּךָ: וְיוֹם הַשְּׁבִיעִי שַׁבָּת לַיהוָה

אֱלֹהֶיךָ לֹא־תַעֲשֶׂה כָל־מְלָאכָה אַתָּה וּבִנְךָ־וּבִתֶּךָ
עַבְדְּךָ וַאֲמָתְךָ וּבְהֶמְתֶּךָ וְגֵרְךָ אֲשֶׁר בִּשְׁעָרֶיךָ:
כִּי שֵׁשֶׁת־יָמִים עָשָׂה יְהוָה אֶת־הַשָּׁמַיִם וְאֶת־הָאָרֶץ
אֶת־הַיָּם וְאֶת־כָּל־אֲשֶׁר־בָּם וַיָּנַח בַּיּוֹם הַשְּׁבִיעִי
עַל־כֵּן בֵּרַךְ יְהוָה אֶת־יוֹם הַשַּׁבָּת וַיְקַדְּשֵׁהוּ: ס
כַּבֵּד אֶת־אָבִיךָ וְאֶת־אִמֶּךָ לְמַעַן יַאֲרִכוּן יָמֶיךָ עַל
הָאֲדָמָה אֲשֶׁר־יְהוָה אֱלֹהֶיךָ נֹתֵן לָךְ: ס לֹא
תִרְצָח: ס לֹא תִנְאָף: ס לֹא תִּגְנֹב: ס לֹא־
תַעֲנֶה בְרֵעֲךָ עֵד שָׁקֶר: ס לֹא־תַחְמֹד בֵּית רֵעֶךָ ס
לֹא־תַחְמֹד אֵשֶׁת רֵעֶךָ וְעַבְדּוֹ וַאֲמָתוֹ וְשׁוֹרוֹ וַחֲמֹרוֹ
וְכֹל אֲשֶׁר לְרֵעֶךָ: פ

"That looks like the Ten Commandments," Danny said. "You know about *that*, right?"

Emma pouted, placed her hands on her hips, and began to recite: "Thou shalt not murder. Thou shalt not steal. Thou shalt not . . ." She was stumped. "Lie?"

Danny shook his head in pity for her ignorance, which fetched him a punch in the arm. "Hey!" he cried. "Thou shalt not sock your best friend!"

"Keppy's my best friend," Emma declared. "Where *is* she? Danny, did you let her get the scarf again?"

Danny shrugged. "Maybe if she makes a little rip in it . . ."

"Danny!"

He left the room, calling Keppy's name.

The two stacks of Hebrew letters were still displayed on the monitor, with one phrase flashing on and off, highlighted in heavy black letters like a headline in a newspaper. If Danny was right and these were the Ten Commandments, Emma figured, then the flashing phrase was the Third Commandment. *No, wait a minute, Hebrew goes from right to left. So that's the Eighth Commandment.* Emma sat and began to copy the weird letters onto a piece of paper. Maybe she could get a head start in learning to write Hebrew. She imagined herself sitting in Danny's Hebrew school for the first time, wearing Vanessa's red scarf and her own jet-black cardigan sweater.

The Ten Commandments vanished from the screen. "Hey!"

HI, EMMA!

"C'mon," she said. "Bring back the Ten Commandments."

They reappeared, with the eighth now in very large letters. At the bottom of the screen the Mitzvah Machine said:

THE EIGHTH: IT MEANS, ''YOU SHALL NOT STEAL.''

Emma's pencil point snapped. Her heart was pounding hard. "I'm not stealing," she said. "The dog took it." *Look at me—I'm talking to a machine. I must be going crazy.*

A new message rolled onto the screen.

LOOK UP IN TORAH: DEUTERONOMY 22:1

"Danny? Come here!"

"Uch," he replied from outside the door, "this dog of yours sure knows how to drool!"

The Mitzvah Machine went blank as soon as Danny entered

the room. "Is the scarf okay?" Emma asked, anxiously unfolding it to full size for an inspection.

"Ahh, she probably has a billion of them."

"No, I have to return it right now." Emma threw the scarf over her shoulder and opened her closet door to get her cardigan. A glance into her wardrobe mirror revealed how handsomely the scarlet fabric complemented the chestnut highlights of her ponytail. "I'll just wear it on the way," she decided, draping the scarf around her neck. "Maybe when I offer to take it off . . ."

"It looks great," Danny said. Emma smiled at him in the mirror. The Mitzvah Machine screen was flickering on her desk behind him.

It was not unusual for Emma to visit the Tribles, yet she felt nervous as she said goodbye to Danny and rode the elevator to the sixth floor. She knew that Vanessa would thank her enthusiastically for returning the scarf, probably offer her milk and cookies, and tell her how she wished she had a daughter like Emma—and all the while Emma would feel guilty and horrible because she had really wanted to keep the scarf for herself.

"Oh, hello, sweetheart," said Vanessa at her door. "Your father is here."

"He is?"

Bruce Levine was slumped in an armchair in the living room. He was wearing his work clothes, a denim shirt, carpenter pants, and plaster-spattered workboots. "Hi, Pop. Are we having supper here or something?" She glanced at the big pendulum clock that hung over the couch: 4:25. Emma knew that Vanessa, who designed fabrics for a living, often worked at home, but as for her father: "How come you're home so early?"

He looked at Emma through tired eyes. "I lost my job

today, Em. This big contract fell through and—oh, what's the use of telling the whole story again? There's no work for now, that's all."

Great! Emma thought carelessly. *Now he can take me to Danny's Hebrew school—maybe even tomorrow!* "Are we eating here?" she asked again.

"Well, we're not eating out, I can tell you that," Bruce replied, rising to his feet. Emma suddenly realized what her father's news meant: no job, no money. *No money, no Hebrew school.*

"Is Mom home yet?" Bruce asked as they rode up in the elevator.

"Uh-uh," Emma said. "Who's cooking?"

"I am," he said, squeezing the back of her neck. "Want to help?"

Emma hunched her shoulders, then gave a little cry as she remembered: the scarf! *I'm still wearing it! Vanessa didn't even notice!*

"Are you okay?" her father asked, thinking he had squeezed too hard.

Emma nodded and skipped down the hallway. She hurried to her room to fold the scarf into her dresser drawer before her mother got home. *Tomorrow I can return it, tomorrow . . .*

The Mitzvah Machine was repeating its last message:

LOOK UP IN TORAH: DEUTERONOMY 22:1

Emma pulled the plug.

Bruce was a carpenter who helped renovate houses and buildings, but his real love was designing and building fine furniture. Sharon, Emma's mom, worked in the billing office of the telephone company, but her real love was playing the piano, which she did well enough to be the accompanist in all of Emma's school plays. Neither of them particularly liked his or her job, and both often daydreamed about other ways to earn a living. Still, they were unhappy about the loss of Bruce's construction job, and evening after evening they would discuss finances, checkbooks, bills, new careers, and so on—conversations that lasted past Emma's bedtime.

She tried to help. She carefully ate everything on her plate, even the slimiest vegetables, so as not to waste food. She offered to give up her allowance and suggested things that the family might sell—the television? her bicycle? the Mitzvah Machine? But her parents always told her not to worry. They had some money saved; they could get by on Sharon's salary for a while; Bruce was sure to find steady work soon enough or perhaps even establish a woodworking shop.

Their confidence was reassuring to Emma, but she didn't have the heart to ask her parents about tuition for Hebrew school—not even when Danny began to nag her each day: "So when are you coming to Beth Shalom? Ask your parents! C'mon, we've got to make you into a real Jew."

He said that again to her as they were playing cards in her room one afternoon. Emma blew up at him. "Stop saying that! I'm as much of a Jew as you or anybody else!"

"Crapola," Danny teased her. "You don't even know what it means. If I had that Mitzvah Machine of yours, I'd be a rabbi by now!"

"You wouldn't even know how to turn it on!"

"Look who's talking! You can't even recite the Ten Commandments!"

"Yeah, and you think you're God because you can!"

Emma's father ducked his curly head into the doorway. "What's happening, friends?"

Danny tried to get rid of him with a "Nothing, sir," but Emma was fuming.

"Danny keeps saying I'm not a real Jew! Just because he goes to Hebrew school!" Then she lowered her eyes to the floor. "Why don't you go home, you big snot?"

"Cut it out, Emma," Bruce warned his sulky daughter.

"Oh, now you're going to blame me!" Emma stamped her foot and plunked down hard on the chair in front of the Mitzvah Machine.

"I'm not blaming anyone," Bruce said, stepping into the room. "In fact, why don't the three of us go to Danny's Hebrew school? We can ask his teacher just how Jewish it is to brag about how much you know."

Danny mumbled an excuse about having to go home. Emma smiled gratefully as her dad winked at her. "Just forget it, Dad," she said. "I don't want to go with *him*. I want to go with *you*."

"Look, Mr. Levine," Danny piped up, waving the paper on which Emma had copied the Eighth Commandment from the Mitzvah Machine. "Emma's a natural!"

Bruce examined his daughter's awkward Hebrew lettering. "Did you write this?" he asked her.

She nodded timidly. "I know you don't have a job, but . . . please, can't we just find out how much it costs? Please?"

Bruce kissed the top of her head. "We're on our way. Put something warm on; there's a nip in the air." He jabbed a finger in Danny's direction. "And you, Mr. 'Real Jew'—you skedaddle!"

"Yahoo!" Danny cried in relief and bolted out of the room.

Emma hurried into her cardigan. She folded the Eighth Commandment paper and shoved it into a pocket. Then she, too, rushed out. Her father was fetching his leather jacket from the hallway closet.

"Whoops," she said, "forgot something."

Vanessa's red chiffon scarf was still lying in the dresser drawer, neatly folded. Emma tied it around her neck and pulled up the collar of her cardigan so that only the red knot showed. Her father wouldn't notice; she wouldn't let her mother see.

Beth Shalom was a small brick building only eight blocks from their apartment house. A glass display sign was mounted at the sidewalk edge of the front lawn, which was carpeted with newly fallen yellow leaves.

Beth Shalom Reform Synagogue
Rabbi Samuel Jacobsen
Hebrew School Instruction:
Mon., Wed., Thurs., 3:30–5:30
Adult Education, Sun., 3–5

How excited she was! And how nervous! Emma wished she could curl up inside her father's jacket pocket instead of passing through the fancy door that he was holding open.

The hallway was dark and hushed. The floor was draped with tarpaulins. "Looks like they're having some work done," Bruce observed.

On the wall facing the doorway was a Joshua tree made of wood and bronze, with small, polished plaques engraved with people's names. Against a side wall was a glass display case containing Hebrew books, a blue-and-white fringed cloth, silver candlesticks, and other silver objects. Emma wondered if her father knew what these things were for—but he was already halfway down the shadowy hall, looking for the synagogue office.

Emma heard a woman's nasal voice: "Can I help you, sir?" Bruce replied too quietly for Emma to hear. "Yes, that would depend on your family income, sir," the woman replied. "Our lowest membership is about four hundred dollars, I believe. I could check for you . . ."

Four hundred dollars! Yikes! That's like going to the movies a hundred times! "Oh, well," Emma said as her father strode back towards her. "I guess that was the shortest conversation in history."

"It's not over yet," Bruce scolded her as they pushed through the doors into daylight. "Your mother and I will talk."

He seemed very glum, which made Emma feel guilty for having asked him to come. She tried to hide her feelings by skipping gaily among the maple leaves that cascaded down the synagogue steps onto the sidewalk.

"Emma," her father said, "those leaves are scattered enough without having you do that."

Then her shuffling foot kicked something. Emma bent and rustled among the leaves until she uncovered a green wallet with lots of compartments and snaps. "Dad . . ."

Bruce examined the compartments. "That's odd," he said, "there's no driver's license, no credit cards . . . just a house key in the change purse and . . . oh, man!" He plucked out a small wad of money and flipped through it, counting. "Unbelievable—three hundred and sixty dollars!"

"I'm rich!" Emma cried, kicking leaves all over the sidewalk. "I'm a millionaire!"

"It's a lot of money," Bruce agreed with a sigh. "That would be most of your tuition right here."

Emma quieted down as she remembered all of the conversations her parents had been having about money, money, money. "No, you take it," she said bravely. "You and Mom. I just want . . . let's see . . . ." She began to wiggle and squirm around as she tried to think of a special wish that wasn't too expensive.

Bruce searched through the wallet again. "There's no identification of any kind." He replaced the bills and snapped the compartment shut. Emma imagined him at the dinner table that evening, taking the money out again to show her mom. "Look at what your brilliant daughter found today." Then he would turn to his brilliant daughter. "I think we can start you in that Hebrew school, no problem!"

She shoved her hands in her pockets and twirled on her toes. Her fingers touched the folded paper on which she had printed the Eighth Commandment, and for a silly second Emma mistook it for a folded-up dollar bill and thought, *More money!* When she remembered what the paper in her pocket really was, Emma stopped her prancing.

THE EIGHTH: IT MEANS, ''YOU SHALL NOT STEAL.''

"Dad? Do you think it belongs to somebody?"

Bruce slipped the wallet into his jacket pocket. "To somebody, of course. To whom, we don't know."

"To a lady, right?"

"It's a woman's wallet," he agreed. "But there's no ID. Let's get home now."

But Emma was glued to the sidewalk, with Vanessa's scarf choking her and with the Mitzvah Machine buzzing like a bee in her ear:

YOU SHALL NOT STEAL!

"Dad!" Reluctantly she followed him. "Daddy!"

"Would you stop whining, please?"

Daddy! It's not our money! You shall not steal! How could she say such a thing to her own father?

"I'm cold," Emma complained.

"How about we go home and get warm?"

"Just a minute." She unwrapped the red scarf and made a grand show of retying it around her neck. "It's lucky I have Vanessa's scarf!"

Bruce beckoned her along. "When did she give it to you?"

Emma remained rooted to her spot. "She didn't."

His beckoning fingers froze.

"She left it at our house," Emma explained with fake cheerfulness. "She doesn't even know it's missing. Finders keepers!"

"What?" Her father charged towards her. "What kind of an attitude. . . !"

Emma hunched her shoulders and ducked her head.

Her father froze in his tracks. He shoved his hands into his pockets and lifted his face to the sky. "I see," he said, nodding.

"Are we going back inside?"

He was still nodding as he took her hand.

A hammering sound echoed through the dark synagogue hallway. "Ouch!" Something clattered to the floor.

Emma scampered towards the commotion. In a room across from the synagogue office she found a plump woman with eyeglasses and short white hair perched on top of a ladder and sucking her bruised thumb. The woman saw Emma and said, "Would you get that hammer for me, please?" The tool had fallen to the floor at the foot of her ladder.

As Emma fetched the hammer the woman spied Bruce in the doorway. "Oh. Well, I can't do this kind of work with people watching." She began to climb down the ladder, then slipped on a rung and barely kept herself from toppling.

Bruce rushed over to steady the ladder. "Let me help. I'm a carpenter."

"You are? Oh, thank goodness!" She grunted as she reached

the floor. "You're a godsend." She pointed to a hole in the wall above the blackboard and handed him a piece of cardboard with some fancy printing on it.

Emma's knees almost buckled when she saw what it said:

DEUTERONOMY 21:10–25:19

''READ IN TORAH, DEUTERONOMY 22:1,'' her Mitzvah Machine had instructed her when she first found Vanessa's lost scarf. "What *is* that?" Emma said.

The woman sucked on her battered thumb again. "What your father's holding? It's the Torah portion we read and study this week. *Ki Tetze*. Beginning with chapter twenty-one, verse ten of Deuteronomy." She smiled at Bruce. "Adult education. Once a week I get to mash my thumbs all over again!"

"It would be a lot easier," he said, "if you'd hang a permanent hook, or shelf. Are you the Hebrew school teacher?"

"Mm-hm. I'm Mrs. G—Dorothy Glickstein."

"Bruce Levine." They shook hands carefully so her thumb would not get squeezed. The effort made them both laugh. "This is my daughter," Bruce said, "Emma Ansky-Levine."

Mrs. G showed Emma a generous smile. "Hello, Emma. I love that red scarf. Are you here to register?"

Emma was still staring at the cardboard in her father's hands. *"Ki Tetze,"* Mrs. G repeated. "It's a Torah portion that contains many, many mitzvot. One of which," she added, shaking her head ruefully, "I wish *somebody* would fulfill: *hashovat aveda*, returning lost property. I lost my wallet today, you see. I don't know where. There was quite a lot of money in it, too. But I'm afraid *hashovat aveda* never gets fulfilled in this city."

Even as Mrs. G was complaining, Bruce drew the green wallet from his jacket pocket.

"Oh, my God!" the teacher shrieked.

"It's yours?"

"Oh, my God! Bless you!" She threw her arms around Bruce and kissed his cheek. "Bless you! Where did you find it?"

"Emma found it," he said, "right in the leaves outside the synagogue."

"I must have dropped it while I was changing the display!"

"By the way," he advised, "there's no identification in it, which doesn't make it any easier to fulfill that mitzvah of yours."

"Oh, well, you see," Mrs. G said, "I lost my ID just last week. I would probably lose my head if it weren't attached to my neck!"

"Excuse me?" Emma interrupted their chitchat. "What does it say in Deuter . . . Deuteronomy twenty-two: one?"

"A living miracle before her eyes," Mrs. G exclaimed, "and she's wondering about the *sidrah*! Well, good for you; let's check." Mrs. G walked across the room and plucked a book off a shelf. "Now, let's see, what did you ask about? Deuteronomy . . . twenty-two . . . one." She read the passage out loud: " 'If you see your fellow's ox or sheep gone astray, do not ignore it; you must take it back to your fellow. . . .' " Mrs. G beamed a smile at Emma. "That's it, dear: *hashovat aveda*. Tell me, are you enrolled in any sort of Jewish school?"

Emma shook her head and found her way to a chair. "Actually," Bruce volunteered, "we did come to see about enrolling Emma with you. She's decided to become bat mitzvah—all on her own. No pressure from us."

"Wonderful!" Mrs. G cried, slamming shut the Torah. "Ouch!" She had caught her sore thumb inside!

Bruce stifled his laughter. "The thing is, the tuition is a little, uh, expensive for us. For now, at least."

"Oh, no!" Mrs. G laid her book carefully on a rung of the ladder. "No no no no. Money is no object when it comes to Jewish education. I'll make you an offer, Mr. Levine: You teach me how to swing a hammer and I'll teach your girl to read a Torah portion. Did you see what's going on in that hallway?"

Bruce nodded. "Renovations."

"The whole synagogue's being done over! Believe me, there's plenty of work for you to exchange for Emma's tuition."

Bruce stepped behind Emma's chair. "What do you think, kiddo?"

"Classes begin in two weeks, right after the High Holy Days," Mrs. G noted, then knelt before Emma. "Emma? Your father would be working very hard for this. Are *you* ready to work hard?"

Emma was holding Mrs. G's *Ki Tetze* cardboard in one hand; from her other hung Vanessa's scarf. She handed both objects to Bruce, then tilted back in her chair. "Ready or not," she announced.

Mrs. G squealed for fear that Emma would fall over backwards. But her father was right there, propping her up. "No problem," Emma reassured her new teacher. "He's got me."

"We've got each other," Bruce said, and nudged her chair upright. *Clunk!*

3

A Flash of Lightning

*T*hunder rolled across the brick walls of Emma Ansky-Levine's apartment building. Emma opened her eyes in the darkness of her bedroom. The huge snake that had been choking her in her dream slithered beneath her bed, to wait until she would fall back to sleep. *How long until morning?* Emma turned to see the illuminated clock on her dresser.

Two glowing marbles were floating in the air only inches from her bedside. Warm, wet breath bathed Emma's face. It was Keppy the Enormous Dog, sitting very close and watching her.

"Are you afraid of the thunder?" Emma whispered. Keppy's tail thumped against the floor. Emma patted the bed and moved closer to the wall. "Come." Keppy lifted her front paws onto the mattress. Lightning flashed, and thunder cracked again. Keppy vaulted up and rested her broad muzzle on Emma's lap.

Raindrops began to patter like a hundred fingers against the windowpane. Again lightning flashed through the darkness of the room, as if the sky were taking a flashcube photograph of Emma and her dog. Thunder broke, and Keppy whimpered. "Shh, it's okay. You're a good girl. Let's see how close the storm is, okay? After the lightning, we count until we hear

35

the thunder." Emma knew that sound takes longer than light to travel through the air; for every five seconds of counting between the lightning and thunder, the storm would be one mile away.

She stroked Keppy's soft ears until the lightning flashed again. Then she turned to watch the sweeping second hand on her clock.

Wait! The Mitzvah Machine was glowing!

"Who turned you on?" Emma whispered. She remembered plugging in the Mitzvah Machine before going to bed so that she could tell it that she had returned Vanessa's scarf. But then she had felt completely ridiculous to be apologizing out loud to a machine and she had yanked the plug—hadn't she?

Her feet felt tender on the wooden floor as she walked to her desk. The room shuddered with light again, and the thunder boomed almost immediately. The storm was so close that she could feel its electrical energy in her room.

SHALOM, EMMA!

"It's a little late, don't you think?" she muttered, staring at the screen.

READ IN TORAH: EXODUS 19:16

"We don't have a Torah and you know it. Let me go back to sleep."

The monitor blinked and filled with words:

EXODUS 19:16
ON THE THIRD DAY, AS MORNING DAWNED, THERE WAS
THUNDER, AND LIGHTNING, AND A DENSE CLOUD UPON
THE MOUNTAIN, AND A VERY LOUD BLAST OF THE HORN;
AND ALL THE PEOPLE WHO WERE IN THE CAMP

TREMBLED. MOSES LED THE PEOPLE OUT OF THE CAMP
TOWARD GOD, AND THEY TOOK THEIR PLACES AT THE
FOOT OF THE MOUNTAIN.

Emma could understand every word, but she couldn't figure
out what the machine could be wanting from her in the middle
of the night.

Next it scrolled out the Hebrew letters of the Ten Commandments in two columns on the screen.

"Right. The Ten Commandments. So?"

Suddenly a huge clap of thunder jolted her building. Emma's
legs buckled beneath her. Keppy began to whimper again.
The monitor read:

YOU SHALL HAVE NO OTHER GODS
BESIDES ME.

Emma was huddled on the floor in front of the glowing
Mitzvah Machine. "Are you . . . are you God?" she peeped,
then cupped her forehead. "What am I, crazy?" She could
just imagine herself taking the machine apart with a screw-
driver: Out would come God, like a genie from a lamp. *But
maybe it's not so crazy,* Emma thought, wondering about
all the weird things the machine had done since coming into
her house: helping her to feed the Mayor, forcing her to
return Vanessa's scarf, getting her enrolled in Hebrew
school. . . .

Lightning flashed again. Thunder cracked as the screen went
dark. Emma leaped back into bed and buried her face in
Keppy's fur.

In the morning the Mitzvah Machine monitor was blank.
The air outside was cool, and the street looked clean and

nearly dry. "Keppy," she said to her sleeping dog, "did it storm last night?" Keppy lifted her head and licked Emma's nose. Emma climbed out of bed and hurried from her room, afraid even to check the Mitzvah Machine's plug.

Her mother had cooked two eggs for Emma to eat. "They're so yellow," Emma observed, staring at her plate. "They look like two little suns."

"Egg eyes," said Sharon, munching a piece of toast. "Sit and eat."

"Mom? Did it rain last night?"

"I'll say. Did the thunder bother you?"

Emma shook her head. "Mom?" she said after a moment. "Do we have a Torah?"

"Not a Hebrew Bible, no," Sharon replied. "I think we have a Bible of some kind in the bookcase in the living room." She leaned closer to her daughter. "First Hebrew school, now Torah—you're getting very interested in being Jewish all of a sudden, aren't you?"

Emma saw two tiny images of herself in her mother's dark eyes. "Sort of," Emma said, unsure of how her mother felt about "being Jewish."

Sharon kissed her forehead. "We haven't taught you very much in that department. Maybe you'll be able to teach us a thing or two."

"Mom?"

"Em?"

"Do we believe in God?"

Sharon sipped from her coffee cup. "That's a big question first thing in the morning."

"Well, do we?"

Again her mother leaned forward. "I believe in you, honey. I believe in people. And if people were made in God's image, as the Bible says, then I guess I believe in God, too." She pointed towards the living room. "There's another book in that bookcase, bottom shelf, called *The Birth of a Child*. Go get it—a big, flat book. Hurry, now, I don't want to be late for work and I don't want you missing your school bus."

The book was all about the development of babies inside their mothers' wombs. Emma was afraid that the pictures would be full of blood and hair and body parts, but her mother turned the pages with such interest that Emma, fidgeting by Sharon's chair, was curious to look.

"Here, this one," Sharon said of a full-page photograph. "What does that look like to you?"

"Sort of like an astronaut," Emma observed.

"Only the astronaut's not wearing a space suit, hm? The astronaut's not wearing anything! It's a fetus," Sharon explained, "just a few weeks before birth, inside a woman's body. Your father gave me this book when I was pregnant with you, and when I saw this picture, how inside my own body it looked so much like outer space, with the stars and planets—do you see what I mean? Well, at that moment . . ."—Sharon closed the book with a sigh—"I believed in God. And God, I believe, is one heck of an artist! Now, eat your breakfast."

"How do they take pictures like that, inside the body?" Emma asked.

"God knows," Sharon replied. "Isn't technology incredible?"

Emma nodded, wondering if her Mitzvah Machine was listening from her bedroom. "Mom? Last night . . . you know Uncle Izzy's computer?"

"Eat," her mother insisted. "We can talk more tonight."

As Emma approached the bus stop, she saw Danny Rosen hovering near Deborah Schott, one of her least favorite people.

Deborah was wearing an antique wool jacket with real fur trim and fur-cuffed boots. She had a small, natural beauty mark under her lip. *She thinks she's Madonna or something.* Emma was eager to tell Danny the latest about the Mitzvah Machine, but she hesitated, expecting that Danny would be in an obnoxious mood as he tried to impress Deborah.

The bus was like a circus train as it pulled up to the curb, with kids shouting and jumping among the seats. Danny joined the other boys, pushing and hollering as they waited for the doors to open. Deborah hung back from the crush, as did Emma. "They're such animals!" Deborah said haughtily.

Emma was watching a flock of pigeons flying overhead, turning and diving in perfect unison. "I guess we're all just a bunch of animals," she replied. "I mean, human beings are a kind of monkey, right? You want to sit with me?" Emma found herself asking.

Deborah shrugged. Emma wondered if she felt insulted at being called a monkey.

"Were you awake during the thunderstorm last night?" Emma said.

Deborah shook her head.

"It sounded like God was taking a walk through the neighborhood," Emma said. "Deborah . . . do you believe in God?"

Deborah glanced sharply at Emma. "Uh-huh," she said, nodding slowly, "and in Mickey Mouse, too."

Richie Finestone came running up to the bus stop. "Hi, Rich," Deborah called to him in a musical voice, then went over and whispered into his ear. Emma heard him say "You're kidding," and then they snickered.

Emma felt mortified. *I better be careful,* she thought, *or I'm going to get a reputation for being weird.* After all, she herself wasn't "religious." She never officially prayed, her family never went to synagogue or lit Sabbath candles, and when she saw, on Saturday mornings, girls in dresses and kneesocks and boys in suits as they walked to and from synagogue, she usually felt sorry for them.

Talk about feeling sorry: the only empty seat on the bus by the time Emma got on was next to Reba Klein, the worst-looking girl in the neighborhood. Reba was a runt, with oily, pimply skin, greasy hair, thick glasses, and a voice that sounded like a siren even in a quiet conversation—and Reba didn't often have quiet conversations, for very few kids ever spoke to her. "If only she was a genius, or a great artist or something," Emma remembered once saying to Danny.

"Yeah, then she'd have some excuse for living" had been Danny's reply.

"Hi," Emma said, sitting and glancing at the girl's hairy forearm.

Reba didn't even look up. Emma found herself thinking of animals again, animals in the zoo who lie in their cages and don't even bother to look at all the gawking people.

"How are you doing?" Emma said.

Reba peeked at her from the corner of her thick glasses. "Fine."

Emma settled more comfortably onto the seat. "Were you awake during that storm last night?"

Reba responded with the slightest nod. She seemed suspicious that Emma was going to turn this supposedly friendly conversation into a put-down.

"You were?" Emma said.

Reba nodded again, then took off her glasses and rubbed her eyes. "It was hard to sleep."

The sight of Reba without glasses created in Emma's mind a whole vision of Reba at home, Reba in her room, Reba in her pajamas, Reba without all the other teasing kids around. *She has a whole life, just like all of us, all the time. . . .*

"I couldn't sleep, either," Emma said. "The thunder was really close to my building. I love the way everything gets lit up all of a sudden."

Reba slipped her glasses back on and again glanced shyly at Emma, who smiled and thought: *What makes a pimple ugly, really? It's just a red bump, unless you think: Ugh! A pimple! Maybe we should call them polka dots.* "Reba, can I ask you something weird? Do you believe in God?"

Reba began to kick her foot against the wall of the bus. "Is this a joke?" she asked in her shrill voice.

"No, I promise. Really. Do you believe in God? I mean, do you ever, more than *believe.* . . ?"

Reba gave a quick little nod.

"You do?" Emma said excitedly. "Tell me!"

The girl spoke into her lap. "I don't know. Sometimes if you close your eyes . . ." She pushed her slipping glasses back onto her nose. "It's like hearing music. It's invisible, but you know it's there. You just can't see it. Sometimes that's how I think . . ."—she tried to soften her siren voice— "about God. . . ."

Emma was dying to tell Reba about the Mitzvah Machine! "So you don't think God would have to look like a person, right?"

All at once a fistful of spitballs hailed on the girls' heads from behind. "Hey!" Emma shouted, vaulting up to find out who had thrown them.

Richie Finestone and Deborah were giggling three rows back. Danny Rosen was sitting across the aisle from Deborah and shaking his head sorrily. Behind him, Robbie Krieger had a faraway look in his eyes that was a sure giveaway. "Robert," Emma said, "you're even a bigger creep than I thought."

"At least I don't sit next to mutants," he retorted.

The bus hit a bump. Emma lurched and grabbed the side of her seat. "Sit down with your mutant, Emmy dear," Robert sassed her.

"You better shut up!" she said.

"You better shut up!" he mimicked her in a nasal, singsong voice.

Emma glared at Danny, who would not meet her eyes.

She turned to sit. Another ball of paper hit her in the back of her head. She pretended not to feel it.

You are a jerk, said the note that Emma passed to Danny while attendance was taken in their classroom.

Sorry, said his reply.

I *hate* Debby Schott!! she wrote back. How can you stand her?

Danny replied: I'm in love. I wish she was in our class.

Emma pretended to be barfing. Then she wrote: I wish Reba was in our class.

It was Danny's turn to gag.

Their homeroom teacher, Mrs. Gayle, caught him at it. "You'll choke worse when you see your report card, Danny, I'm warning you."

"Sorry," he said, blushing.

"If you and Emma are finished being pen pals, it's time for the Pledge of Allegiance."

The class stood amidst a clatter of sliding chairs. "I pledge allegiance to the flag of the United States of America, and to the Republic for which it stands, one nation, under God . . ."

Emma remained standing after the pledge was recited. "Mrs. Gayle?"

"Yes, Emma?"

"What does it mean, 'one nation, under God'?"

Mrs. Gayle balled her hands on the desk in front of her. "I would guess that it means something different to each person. Would you like to say what it means to you?"

Emma glanced over at Robbie Krieger, whose desk was by the window. He sneered and wrapped his arms across his chest. "Well, I'm not sure," Emma said. "I think for a lot of people God is up in the clouds, so we're 'under God.'"

A few of her classmates laughed. "I'm serious!" Emma protested.

Mrs. Gayle stepped over to the blackboard to command the class's attention. She asked Emma to sit. Emma obeyed but raised her hand.

"Yes, Emma. Do you want to try again?"

She popped back up. "Sometimes, like before a test? I see kids praying to God, who they can't even see—but meanwhile, every day they treat other kids who are standing right in front of their noses like they're a bunch of . . . of . . ."

"Mutants," Robbie Krieger muttered.

"Mr. Krieger!" cried Mrs. Gayle. "Have you something to add to this discussion?"

"Uh-uh, not me," Robbie said, slumping in his chair.

"Emma," Mrs. Gayle said, turning back to her, "there is something in this country called the separation of church and state, which makes it very difficult to talk about religious matters in the classroom. I think the question you're concerned with is a good one—but perhaps it should be dealt with elsewhere."

Emma nodded glumly and sat down, wondering: *How come talking about God seems to drive people crazy?*

"My Mitzvah Machine thinks it's God," Emma told Danny as they trudged from the bus stop to their twin apartment buildings at the end of the day.

"Your Mitzvah Machine is wrong," Danny said. "Deborah Schott is God."

"Danny," she pleaded, stamping her foot, "will you stop being a jerk? If I can't talk about this to you, there's nobody left but Keppy! I'm telling you, the Mitzvah Machine thinks it's God!" Then she told him about the strange behavior of the machine during the thunderstorm. "The last thing it said," Emma concluded, "just before that last thunderbolt that made me so scared I was ready to die!—the last thing it said was something like, 'You shall have no other gods besides me.' "

Danny's jaw dropped—and so did the rest of him, onto the sidewalk, where he lay giggling and rolling while Emma kicked him and yelled, "What's so funny? *What's so funny?*"

"That's the Second Commandment, you dummy!" he said at last. "Your computer was just giving you a lesson in the middle of the night."

Emma stared at him distrustfully.

"Look, get it straight," Danny said, sitting up. "God gave the Ten Commandments to all the Hebrew people in the desert at Mount Sinai. You will not murder, you will not steal . . ."

"To *all* the people? Not just to Moses?"

"All of them," Danny repeated. "It says in the Bible, they were all there, and God spoke right to 'em." Danny bent back one finger at a time as he recited: "You will not lie— like, as a witness, you've got to tell the truth. You're not supposed to get jealous of what your neighbor's got; you're supposed to keep the Sabbath; you're supposed to honor your mother and your father; you're not supposed to commit adultery—no matter what they tell you on television!; you're not supposed to use 'God' as a swearword or say it to be cool; and you're not supposed to build idols, which is the Second Commandment: 'You shall have no other gods . . .' "

"I see." She kicked the sole of Danny's sneaker. "What about Deborah Schott?"

Danny scrunched up his face in bewilderment. "What *about* her?"

"She's your idol, isn't she?"

"Oh, c'mon, I was just kidding about that."

Emma slowly shook her head. "When aren't you kidding, Danny?" she said. "If God came to visit you in *your* bedroom, what would you do, tell a dumb joke about Reba Klein?"

"No!" he replied. "But I also wouldn't think God was living inside my computer!"

"Of course *you* wouldn't!" Emma cried. "You're one of those idiots who believes we're 'under God.' " She thrust her thumb skywards. "God's only up in the sky, right?" She patted her heart. "Not in here." She tapped her temple. "Not in here. And *certainly* not within a hundred yards of Reba Klein!"

"Hey," Danny said with a shrug, "maybe God's got a thing for mutants."

"Uch! I don't want to be your friend anymore," Emma declared, and stalked away towards her building.

"Oh, come *on*, would you please?"

"You just don't get it, do you?" she shouted back at him.

"Emma!" He picked himself up from the sidewalk. "Give me a break; I was only kidding! Emma!"

4

The Flow of the River

Dear Uncle Izzy,

I've had the Mitzvah Machine for just over three weeks.
It's already taught me a lot. For a while I was scared
of the way it seems to talk to me, and I even started
talking back. Also, it came on in the middle of the night,
which was weird. I wanted to tell my mom and dad
about some of the things it was doing, but I never got
the chance until yesterday, during supper, when I told
them how it's broken. The screen's lit up, but there aren't
ever any messages. Dad tried messing with it, but then
he said I should write to you and ask how to get it to
work again. I'm starting Hebrew school right after the
High Holy Days, and I really want the Mitzvah Machine
to do whatever it's supposed to be doing to help me.

The last time it said anything was during a
thunderstorm. It showed the Ten Commandments in
Hebrew and began to translate the one about God being
the only god there is. Like I said, this was the middle
of the night, and to tell the truth, I got pretty scared.
The next day at school (my regular school) I started
asking everyone about God, and I was getting into trouble
just by talking about it, and my friend Danny Rosen
and I broke up. (He wasn't my boyfriend or anything,
but we used to hang around together.)

I guess this letter sounds pretty ungrateful. I meant
to be writing a thank-you note, but, to be honest, so

49

*far the Mitzvah Machine is not much fun. It doesn't
play any kind of games or anything, and every time it
shows a message, bizarre things happen. It's making me
think a lot about being Jewish, but it was really Danny
who made me think about that, because his family's
observant and he's always saying that I don't know
anything about Judaism. And now Danny's not saying
anything to me (really, I'm not talking to him) and neither
is the Mitzvah Machine!*

Emma put down her pen and read what she had written. It
sounded immature and whiny to her. She crumpled the paper
and threw it into her wastebasket. She was in a terrible mood.

Staring out the window, she saw a few families, the Rosens
among them, walking past the hill between apartment buildings on their way to Beth Shalom. It was the morning of
Rosh Hashanah, the Jewish New Year. School was closed,
and Emma was glad to be at home in her pajamas—yet she
also wondered what everyone would be doing at Beth Shalom.
She tried to beam her thoughts at Danny: *Fatso, jerk, why
don't you trip over your own feet?* He walked safely out of
her view.

She looked at the Mitzvah Machine's sea of green light.
"Tell me about Rosh Hashanah," she commanded. The screen
flickered and remained blank. "Please!" she whined. Then
she wrote on a new piece of paper: *"Dear Uncle Izzy, thank
you for the Mitzvah Machine. Is there a manual or something
that you can send me?"*

"There's a big brown dog in the living room waiting to
be walked!" called her mother through Emma's door.

"Okay, okay," Emma replied, and quickly got dressed.

She and Keppy reached the lobby of the building just as
Sandra, the mail carrier, was filling up mailboxes. Sandra
greeted her sweetly and reached into her leather pouch to
hand the girl a postcard—from Israel! From Uncle Izzy!

"I was just writing to him!" said Emma.

"I guess you must be on the same wavelength," Sandra said, and continued to sort the mail as Keppy pulled Emma away, through the lobby towards the front door.

The illustration on the postcard was an old woodcarving showing Jewish men in prayer shawls standing by a river. *"Tashlich,"* it said in little print on the back of the card. "A ritual of the Jewish New Year, Rosh Hashanah, when Jews throw bread crumbs onto flowing water to symbolize the casting away of sins." In his trim, tiny handwriting, Uncle Izzy had written,

Dear Emma,

By now I'm sure you've figured out how the Mitzvah Machine operates, but if ever it were to go on the blink, try cutting an onion in the same room and see what happens.

L'Shanah Tovah—
Uncle Izzy

An onion! He must be kidding, Emma thought as she walked Keppy around the neighborhood. *Funny how he wrote to me just while I was going to write to him. It's like all those stories you hear about how so-and-so telephoned so-and-so just when the second so-and-so was thinking about the first so-and-so—mental telepathy!*

She and Keppy had gone about a block from her apartment building, to a shady street of private houses, when Emma heard shouts. Keppy tensed and growled. Emma held the leash tight and stood watching a grown man slapping a girl in a doorway. The girl was silent, with her head ducked under her arms as the man yelled and pounded her.

Finally he gave the girl a shove against the porch railing and entered the house, slamming the door behind him.

The girl immediately lowered her arms and fixed her hair. Her eyes were black with smudged mascara.

"Deborah?" said Emma. Yes, it was Deborah Schott!

Deborah's mouth trembled before she put on her usual snooty airs and said, "What are you looking at?"

"Nothing," Emma stammered, "I'm just . . . are you okay?"

"Yeah," Deborah said, "he doesn't hurt."

"Is that your father?" Emma asked in a low voice.

"No! If my father was here, I wouldn't have to—" Deborah cut herself short. "He's my mother's boyfriend." She made her voice sound breathless and adoring: "Ralphie boy. Ooh, Ralphie!"

Emma was afraid the man might be listening at the door. "I'm taking Keppy for a walk," Emma said. "You want to come?"

"Take a hike." Deborah patted her hair once more and reached for the doorknob.

Emma spent the rest of the holiday morning in her room, trying to get the Mitzvah Machine to send her a message. She even followed Uncle Izzy's advice and sliced onions on a cutting board alongside the keyboard until tears were streaming from her stinging eyes.

Nothing happened. "Come on! Why won't you talk to me?" she yelled at the monitor, and slapped her desk.

"Ouch." Emma rubbed her smarting hand and thought about Deborah getting smacked over the head. *Did you see that makeup she was wearing? She probably smokes, drinks— she always thinks she's soooo hot.*

The phone was ringing in the kitchen. Emma ran to wash her hands clean of onion juice before she answered it.

"Emma? It's Danny."

She was startled to hear his voice. "What do *you* want?" she said suspiciously.

"Rabbi Jacobsen," he replied, "said in synagogue that we're supposed to make up with our friends before Yom Kippur—"

Emma broke in: "So what are you calling *me* for?"

"C'mon, Emma," Danny warned, "don't get stuck up. You're the one who broke up with me. You should be doing the calling."

"I didn't break up with you," she said. "I broke up with a jerk. I saw your girlfriend this morning, by the way."

"Who?"

"Deborah. She was getting smacked around by her mother's boyfriend, right in front of her house."

"She told me she gets hit a lot," Danny said sadly.

"Oh? Since when do you talk with Deborah Schott so much?"

"Since I started tutoring her in math."

"What?" Emma squealed. "You're tutoring Deborah Schott?"

"You really can't imagine her paying attention to me, can you?" Danny said. "Just because I'm a little chubby. You think Debby's some kind of superstar and I'm just a drooling fan, right? Let me tell you something, Emma, you've got a lot of nerve getting all stuck up about that mutant Reba."

Emma stiffened with anger, then took a deep breath. "I don't like Deborah Schott," she said.

"You're jealous," Danny insisted.

"Of what? You're not my boyfriend!"

"I'm not talking about me. I'm talking about Finestone. You used to tell me you thought Richie Finestone was the ultimate dream, right? And everyone thinks he and Debby are going out together, right?"

"They're not?"

"Nope. Debby told me they broke up. And she's seeing *me* this afternoon."

"I don't believe it! She's moving from Richie Finestone to you?"

"You see what I mean?" Danny said. "You just can't believe it! Well, come to the park in about an hour and see for yourself—I'm teaching her how to do *tashlich*. You probably don't even know what that means, do you?"

"Yes, I do!" Emma scrambled to find Uncle Izzy's postcard. "It's when you throw bread crumbs onto flowing water to symbolize the casting away of sins."

"Ooh," Danny said sarcastically, "you sound like you're a bat mitzvah already! Say hello to your Mitzvah Machine."

"I can't," Emma said miserably. "It's not—" Then she heard a click. Danny had hung up.

What an awful conversation! He was right, too: She *had* been acting snooty. She had to confess she was missing his company, his jokes, his imitations of their teachers, his horsing around with Keppy. *Who knows?* Emma thought. *Maybe he does have a way of reaching Deborah's heart. I mean, he's basically a sweet, innocent kid. Maybe Debby's able to take off her glamour mask when she's with him, talk about real things.*

"Yeah, right!" Emma muttered to herself. "Deborah's just the type to stand there by the river, talking about everything that's wrong with her, in public!"

Yet that's exactly what everyone was doing, Jews of every kind, as Emma arrived at the park. There were bearded chasidic men in fur hats and black gaberdines; Orthodox women wearing wigs and long dresses; Reform Jews dressed like her mom and dad on a Saturday night; Jews who looked Hispanic, Jews who looked Arabic, Jews who looked Asian—all of them walking quietly in family groups and filing onto the bridge spanning the oily stream that flowed from the rowing pond to who-knew-where. Scores of people, people who looked like they wouldn't even talk to one another on any given day of the year, were here, standing shoulder to shoulder, over the water and under the sky, reading from prayer books and dropping crumbs into the water.

Where was Danny? Emma looked in every direction as she stood at the railing of the bridge amid the buzz of Hebrew. She desperately wanted to find him so that he could teach her, too, how to do *tashlich,* how to be a part of this ceremony, this people, this moment.

A woman behind her was praying in English: "He will take us back in love; He will cover up our iniquities . . . hurl all our sins into the depths of the sea. . . ." Then Emma saw them below! On the rocky bank of the river, just a few yards away from another clump of praying, swaying people, Danny was standing close to Deborah. He had on a gray suit and a white *kippah,* and he was pointing to a page in a book. Deborah was wearing a tight black tube dress and a pink baby-doll sweater; her hand was resting on Danny's shoulder. Emma was tempted to holler their names, but she knew that a loud voice would be inappropriate, jarring to the solemn mood of the crowd. *Danny,* she beamed her thoughts to him, *look up at the bridge! Danny, look up!*

Look up, Danny!

LOOK OUT!

Robbie Krieger had snuck up behind Emma's friend and was down on his hands and knees. Deborah kept nodding, pretending to be listening with deep interest to Danny, meanwhile pressing closer and closer to him until he nervously edged away and—alley oop!—he flipped like a broken doll across Robbie's back and landed in mud.

From the bridge, Emma couldn't hear what Robbie had

to say, but she saw him spring up quickly to his feet and retrieve his own *kippah* from the ground. He offered Danny a hand to help him up. Danny shook his head miserably; Emma could tell that he was holding back tears. Deborah, on the other hand, was holding back her laughter as Robbie shrugged, tossed a few bread crumbs in the water, and sauntered up the hill towards the foot of the bridge.

"It was an accident!" Deborah was insisting as Emma finally arrived at her fallen friend's side. "Robbie dropped his whatchamacallit, his hat."

"Oh, right!" Emma argued. "That was about as much an accident as the slap that guy gave you this afternoon!"

"Mind your business," Deborah sneered at her.

"This is my business!"

"You little twit," Deborah said, then looked down at Danny, still on his butt in the mud. "Are you going to teach me *tashlich*, or are you going to spend the afternoon being a crybaby?"

"You just learned it," he said miserably, and lifted his teary face. "It's like this . . ." His chest heaved. "You get slapped around . . . so then you slap me around . . . and then I pass it along to Reba Klein! It all flows down the river, Deborah! And where do you think it ends up? Huh? Where do you think it ends up?"

"In your fat belly, from the look of it," Deborah said, and sashayed off in the same direction as Robbie Krieger.

"Go to hell!" Danny yelled after her.

Emma took his elbow to help him to stand. The seat of his pants was soaked through.

"She can go to hell," he repeated, his voice cracking. "Oh, God, my prayer book! Look at it, it's all messed up!"

Emma fetched the book for him from the edge of the stream. The binding was broken and the pages were wet and stuck together. "I'll carry it," Emma volunteered, "so you don't get your suit dirty."

"Forget it!" Danny cried. "I'm already a mess—a fat, stupid mess!"

"No, you're not," Emma said, rubbing his shoulder. "You are not. I really like what you said about *tashlich*, Danny. Personally, I think it's Deborah who's the messed-up one. She doesn't even know how to feel sorry, not even for herself!"

Danny sniffled, then managed to laugh. "Well, I sure know how to feel sorry for *my*self! I'm a crybaby from way back!"

"Maybe that's why we have tear ducts," Emma said, "so we can do *tashlich* every day."

"Just what I need!" Danny groaned. "Who taught you that, your Mitzvah Machine?"

5

A Blessing for Rachel

T he Mitzvah Machine began communicating again with a simple ''HELLO!'' that very Rosh Hashanah day when Emma returned from consoling Danny in the park. Somehow she was not surprised; she had begun talking to her best friend again, so it made sense that Uncle Izzy's machine would be talking to her again. Tears from the vapors of an onion had not done the trick, but the tears of *tashlich*, the invisible tears of her heart—to these, she suspected, her Mitzvah Machine would always reply.

"I figured you'd have something to say," Emma told the Mitzvah Machine as she entered her room and heard it humming.

THE TALMUD TELLS US:
''THE HOLY ONE WANTS THE HEART.''

Emma read this and nodded. "I know what you mean— only I don't know what the Talmud is. But I can ask Danny now!" She copied the proverb onto a slip of paper.

Hebrew school classes with Dorothy Glickstein began two weeks later. As Emma's bat mitzvah preparations got under way, the Mitzvah Machine proved to be a fantastic help. It played simple word games using the Hebrew alphabet, which were a lot more fun than her textbook lessons. It outlined the synagogue service in which she would be called to say *berachot*, blessings, over the Torah, so that she could have some idea of what was in store for her. It printed talmudic proverbs and blessings to recite for just about every other occasion, too. Whatever was on Emma's mind, the Mitzvah Machine had something to say about it—something drawn from a Jewish source.

"Emma's very, very bright," Mrs. G told the elderly Rabbi Jacobsen when they were reviewing the progress of her pupils after four months of classes. "She learns so quickly, it's almost frightening. When we began in October, she didn't even know what Torah was!"

"Ignorance is no sin," said Rabbi Jacobsen. "The great Rabbi Akiva himself did not begin to study the Torah until he was forty years old."

"I know, I know," said Mrs. G. "But Emma now *quotes* to us from the Torah, the Talmud, the sages! She carries these little slips of paper from which she reads to us—I've seen them; they're in her own handwriting. And she has real insight into things Jewish! Every time I lead a discussion in class about the meaning of being *b'nai mitzvah*, or about Jewish history, about culture, about anti-Semitism—we try, Samuel, we try to give them more than the *alef-bet* as an education, hm?"

"Good, good," said the rabbi.

"And every time, Emma has something to contribute. It's as if there were a *tsaddik*, a wise one, sitting behind her, whispering things into her ear. It's not her parents, I can tell you that," continued Mrs. G. "You met her father, Bruce Levine—the one who built the cabinets and benches here in the shul?"

"Ah, yes. A nice man."

"A wonderful man," she agreed, "and an excellent carpenter—but as a Jew, he knows nothing."

"Have you met the mother?" Rabbi Jacobsen asked.

"Not yet," she said. "Maybe she's the one who's given her daughter such a Jewish *kop*. But I'll have to wait—next week we begin work on the Purim play, which is going to keep me *very* busy."

"Blessed are you, O Lord our God, Ruler of the universe, who clothes the naked."

Emma recited this blessing before buttoning a blouse that she was trying on at Patchworks, a clothing store in the mall. Her new friend from Hebrew school, Rachel Korn, was trying on clothes in the next dressing room. She whispered to Emma through the wall: "Will you stop mumbling over everything you do? It's so embarrassing!"

"It's just a way of concentrating on what I'm doing," Emma said.

"Since when do you have to concentrate," Rachel said, "just to get dressed? Besides, you're not supposed to say that blessing until you *buy* the clothes."

"That's okay," Emma replied, stepping out to look at herself in a full-length mirror. "Sometimes I even make up my own blessings. It's fun. . . . Uch, I'm so flat-chested!"

"Oh, my God!" Rachel suddenly cried. "Come here!"

Emma rushed over to Rachel's door. She could see her friend from the knees down. Rachel spoke through the door in a low, hoarse voice. "I just got my period for the first time."

"You're kidding!"

"I'm not! I'm trying on these pants, and—"

"But you're not even twelve years old!"

"Do you have any tissues, please?"

Emma hurried back to her cubicle to search her coat pockets. She wanted to feel thrilled for her new friend, but Emma felt more jealous than thrilled. Was there a blessing to say for Rachel? *And for me. Someday soon it'll happen to me. "Blessed are You, Ruler of the universe, who makes girls bleed." Nah, that sounds awful. "Blessed are You who manufactures sanitary napkins. . . ."*
Guess I'll have to ask the Mitzvah Machine.

"Here, Rachel," Emma said as she handed her a clump of tissues through the door. "Now you can go swimming, or horseback riding, or play tennis."

"What are you talking about?" Rachel said in a fretful voice.

"It's a joke," Emma explained. "You know those advertisements for sanitary napkins that show women doing all that stuff? Horseback riding—"

"This is no joke," Rachel said.

"Sorry," Emma replied.

"Mom?" She asked Sharon the next evening. "Why do you think girls become bat mitzvah when they're thirteen?"

Sharon was at the piano, working her way through a difficult composition. "I don't understand the question," she said. "Do you mean, why not when they're twelve, or fourteen?"

Emma nodded. "Supposedly it's about becoming a grown-up, but most of the boys don't seem very grown-up when they're thirteen."

"Girls mature faster," Sharon said.

"We sure do," Emma agreed.

Sharon's fingers hovered above the keys. "Emma," she said, "are you trying to tell me something?"

"Not about me." Emma shook her head dejectedly. "Rachel Korn, from Hebrew school? She got her period for the first time today."

Her mother swung around on the piano bench. "Rachel Korn? Really! She's so young!"

"She won't even be twelve until July!" Emma said, pouting.

"I don't believe how time is racing along!" her mother sighed. "Soon I'll be slapping your cheeks!"

"What do you mean?"

Sharon laughed. "The first time I spotted, my mother gave me two little slaps on the cheek. I don't know why—I don't think she knew, either, just that her mother did it to her. It's a tradition. Until then," Sharon said, holding open her arms for a hug, "a kiss for each cheek."

"I'm not sure that Grandma should have done that," Emma said as her mother embraced her. "I think you're not supposed to touch someone who has her period."

"That's ridiculous," Sharon said, holding her at arm's length. "Who says?"

"The Torah," Emma replied. "It's like, getting your period turns you into some kind of leper, so that you can't be touched."

"Emma! I don't feel that way about menstruation at all!" Sharon cried. "And neither should you! Who told you that?"

Emma shrugged, and then confessed: "The Mitzvah Machine."

"Uncle Izzy's machine? Is *that* what it's filling your head with!"

"It's just quoting from Torah, Mom."

"I don't care if it's quoting from the president of the United States!" Sharon said.

Emma tugged her mother's hand. "Come and see. I've been wanting you to. . . . Come on, please." She could hardly wait to share with her mother all the secrets about the Mitzvah Machine.

IGNORE TORAH, said its monitor as Emma entered her room. But as Sharon followed her in, the screen blanked out.

"Ignore Torah?" Emma said out loud. "It said I should ignore Torah."

"That's probably the first good advice it's given you," Sharon said.

Emma called to her machine: "Talk to my mother, too."

Nothing: just a sea of rippling green light.

Sharon wrapped her arms around her daughter. *"This,"* she said, "is the machine I want you to care about—your body. I want you to love it, honey, through all of its transformations."

"Okay, okay," Emma said, wriggling free.

FORGET ABOUT TORAH, the Mitzvah Machine now had on its screen. "Look!" Emma called to Sharon, just before the monitor went blank again.

The next time her Hebrew class met, Emma asked Mrs. G if there was any reason why a Jew was supposed to "forget about Torah."

The teacher was in the middle of telling the class about the approaching holiday of Purim. It was a holiday, she explained, on which Jews dressed up as characters from the *Megillah,* the Book of Esther, and celebrated the downfall of Haman, the wicked advisor to Queen Esther's husband, King Ahasuerus—Haman, who hated all Jews and tried to have them killed, but was tricked by Esther and her uncle Mordecai. Mrs. G suggested that the class put on a Purim *shpiel,* a performance for their parents or friends. Then Emma asked her question.

"A time to forget about Torah?" Mrs. G replied. "Well . . . I suppose a Jew is supposed to forget about most of the mitzvot if it means saving a life, including one's own. And in general our Reform movement doesn't consider *halachah,* the legal sections of Torah, to be binding on us. Tell me, Emma, what does this have to do with Purim, hm?"

"Well . . . Queen Esther, for instance," Emma replied, thinking on her feet. "When she was with the king—he was still married to Vashti, right? So Esther was committing adultery."

Emma heard some snickering behind her back.

"Those were different times, Emma," Mrs. G said. "Some kings had many wives."

"But the Torah is for all times, isn't it?" Emma said.

"The Torah," Mrs. G said, "doesn't object to polygamy."

"You're kidding!"

"I'm very serious. I'm also a little pressed for time in class today, so why don't you see me right afterwards, Emma. All right?"

Emma nodded and thought, *Maybe she can tell me a blessing for Rachel, too.*

"Emma," Mrs. G said, "I want to begin by saying that you are the most remarkable student to come my way in a very long time. I was wondering if you'd play the role of Queen Esther in our Purim *shpiel*."

Emma was stunned. "Really?"

"After all," Mrs. G said with a smile, "if we're going to spend our time evaluating whether or not Queen Esther's behavior violated the Torah . . ."

"What do I have to do?"

"Ah! You haven't yet read the Book of Esther! Good, there's something left for me to teach you." Mrs. G had the text opened on the table. She began to read out loud: " 'In the fortress Shushan lived a Jew by the name of Mordecai. . . . He was foster father to Hadassah—that is, Esther—his uncle's daughter, for she had neither father nor mother. The maiden was shapely and beautiful . . .' "

Shapely and beautiful. The words slapped Emma in the face. "I don't think I want to," she said.

Ms. G looked up and wrinkled her nose with surprise. "But I haven't told you anything about her! Let's get to the part that you're concerned about, all right? This question of being with King Ahasuerus while he's still married to Queen Vashti . . ." She began to flip clumsily through the pages.

"Mrs. G?" Emma asked.

"Yes, darling?"

"I was wondering . . . is there a blessing for a girl when—"

Emma was interrupted by a ruckus that had arisen in the hallway outside: boys laughing and shouting. When something thudded against the wall, Mrs. G hurried to the doorway with Emma right behind.

They saw Elly Kramer, a big girl just one month away from celebrating her bat mitzvah, in tears. Her blouse was rumpled, tails half out of her pants. Billy Golden and Sam Bank, who were also in training for bar mitzvah, were standing around looking guilty, Sam with his back against the wall.

"What is going on here?" Mrs. G demanded to know.

"We were just playing around," Billy said.

Emma somehow knew from what she saw and heard that the "playing around" had to do with Elly's body, with the fact that she was wearing a bra. Mrs. G must have had the same idea, for she was furious. "I'm going to find out what happened," she told the sulking boys, "and then I'll be speaking to your parents! Now, out of here, both of you!"

The boys shuffled away. "Are you okay?" Emma quietly asked Elly.

Elly was annoyed, not hurt. "They kept calling me 'Vashti' and snapping my bra!"

" 'Vashti'!" Mrs. G cried. "Oh, this is intolerable! Intolerable!" She beckoned them both into the classroom and closed the door. "Elly, darling," she said, "do you remember who Vashti is?"

"She was King Ahasuerus's wife," Elly recalled. "When the king was drunk with some friends one night, he ordered her to dance naked in front of them. And she wouldn't," Elly said.

"Good for her," Emma cheered.

"So the king punished her," Elly said, "and married Esther instead."

"Mrs. G!" Emma declared. "I definitely do *not* want to be Esther in the play!"

Mrs. G patted her hand. "You're not going to be, darling," she said. "You're going to be King Ahasuerus instead."

"What?" Emma yelped.

"And one of those boys," the teacher said, turning to Elly, "is going to be Vashti!"

Elly's eyes lit up at the idea.

"And a boy," Mrs. G continued, "is going to play Queen Esther! And a girl is going to play her uncle, Mordecai! We're going to take the *Megillah* and stand it on its head."

The Mitzvah Machine's words came back to Emma: *Ignore Torah. Forget about Torah.*

Dorothy Glickstein seemed to read her mind: "That question you asked in class, Emma, about forgetting the Torah? Well, sometimes you have to forget the Torah in order to fulfill the Torah. I've always wondered why God's name is not mentioned in the *Megillah,* not even once!" she added. "Now I'm beginning to understand. The story's all about how human beings sometimes have to change the rules." She smiled at both girls. "Trust me. It's going to be the best Purim *shpiel* in the history of Beth Shalom!"

The boys in the class were outraged when Mrs. G assigned them female roles during the first rehearsal of their Purim *shpiel.* "I'm not going to go dancing around like a jerk!"

protested Billy Golden, who was to play Queen Vashti.

"Oh, yes, you are!" commanded Emma as King Ahasuerus. "Dance, Vashti!"

"The girls don't really *count* in this story," said Marvin Wertheimer, who was to play Queen Esther. "I mean, my whole job is just to *beg* the king not to kill the Jews!"

"Start begging!" commanded King Ahasuerus.

"This is not how the story is supposed to go!" Billy argued again. "You're making it up! There's nothing in the Bible that says boys should play girls."

King Ahasuerus replied: "Forget Torah! And thank you, God, for letting us be creative!"

"Amen," said Mrs. G from the front of the room. "Amen, Your Highness!"

As her teacher applauded, Emma realized that she had done it, quite by accident: she had created a blessing for Rachel Korn. *Blessed are You, Ruler of the universe, who allows us to be creative. Blessed are You, Lord our God, who allows us to create. Blessed are You, Lord our God, who allows us to create new life. Blessed are You, God, dear God, who allows us to be women.*

"Dance, Vashti!" commanded King Ahasuerus.

6

Numbers

When Danny phoned Emma on the Memorial Day weekend to ask her to visit Deborah Schott in the hospital with him, Emma's reply was "I'm too busy."

It was no lie. She was busily studying her new volume of the Torah, which was spread open on her desk to the *sidrah* for the week of her bat mitzvah, *Ki Tavo*. She was terribly anxious about being prepared for that day, only four months away, and was taking advantage of the three-day holiday weekend to buckle down.

"Please come," Danny begged her. "I've never been in a hospital before."

"Deborah Schott is not my favorite person," Emma said coldly. "Anyway, we already wrote her letters from school."

"Oh, big deal!" Danny cried. "No one even mentioned *why* she's in the hospital! Everyone writes, 'I hope you get better soon'—as if she's sick."

"She *is* sick," Emma said. "Her whole family's sick!"

"But she doesn't have a disease, Emma!" Danny replied. "Her mother's boyfriend punched her out!"

"Knowing her," Emma muttered, "she probably deserved it."

"Oh, Emma! How can you say that?"

"It's true! Listen to this, Danny: 'If you do not obey the

Lord your God to observe faithfully all His commandments and laws which I enjoin upon you this day, all these curses shall come upon you and take effect . . .' "

"What are you reading?"

"The Torah portion for the week of my bat mitzvah! I may try to learn some of the Hebrew."

"You're a fanatic, you know that?" Danny said. "I'm sorry I ever told you about Hebrew school!"

"*You're* the fanatic!" Emma retorted. "How can you still have a crush on her, after she was so mean to you?"

"You don't have to *like* somebody to visit them when they're sick!" he replied. "It's a mitzvah, Emma! *Bikkur cholim.* Go and ask your stupid Mitzvah Machine!"

"It's also a mitzvah to study," Emma said. "And that's what I have to do."

"Just come with me to the hospital," Danny pleaded again. "You don't even have to come into her room! Come on, it's Memorial Day!"

"What does *that* have to do with anything?"

"It's about being a good citizen."

"Wrong!" Emma scoffed. "It's about useless wars!"

"Emma . . ."

"Look, Danny, I'm too busy, I really am."

"Okay, thanks a lot," he said, and ended their argument by hanging up.

Within seconds, Emma heard a knock on her door. "What?"

"I hope you're not too busy," said her mother, "to take this beast out for a holiday stroll."

"Just a minute," Emma said, annoyed that her mother had eavesdropped on her conversation.

As Keppy tugged her around the neighborhood, Emma wondered if she'd be able to keep on studying as hard as she

had all winter. It was one thing to spend afternoons in front of the Mitzvah Machine when the sun set early and the frigid nights made indoors the place to be. But Memorial Day marked the beginning of holiday time: the days were lengthening and warming up, and the flowers were saying hello, hello, hello.

I wonder if there are any flowers in Debby's hospital room. What exactly happened to her? Mrs. Gayle had only reported to the class that Deborah was "injured." Richie Finestone had spread the word that it was her mother's boyfriend who had done the injuring. But the rumors about Deborah's condition ranged from "her mascara smudged" to "he broke every bone in her body."

Slam bam whack whap! Emma remembered vividly the sight of "Ralphie boy" raining blows on the girl's head.

"Keppy!" The dog was straining at her leash. Before Emma could call her to heel, an elderly, bearded man who was walking in front of them had the taut cord pressed against the back of his knees. He fell backwards onto the sidewalk with a thud. Keppy proceeded to slobber all over him.

"Rabbi Jacobsen!" Emma recognized him even as he raised his hands to ward off the dog's licking tongue. "Omigod, Rabbi Jacobsen, I'm so sorry! Keppy! Stop! What's wrong with you?" Emma landed her foot in Keppy's rump and forced her into a sitting position.

"Shh, don't kick," the rabbi said.

"She deserves it! You bad dog, Keppy! You stay put now!" Keppy ducked her head and flattened her ears sadly.

"She likes rabbis instead of rabbits, your dog," Rabbi Jacobsen said as he took hold of the hand that Emma was offering to help him up.

She was small for the job. The sleeves of Rabbi Jacobsen's jacket slid way up on his arms as Emma tugged. She saw blue tattoo marks above his right wrist.

The rabbi noticed her staring. "As you see," he said, "I've met worse beasts than your dog." He adjusted his sleeve to cover the tattooed numbers. "You're the girl with the *Yiddishe kop,* from Mrs. Glickstein's class?"

Emma nodded, awed by what she had just seen. She hadn't known that Rabbi Jacobsen was a Holocaust survivor!

"Your teacher tells me you're becoming a real Torah master," the rabbi said.

"I wish," Emma replied.

Rabbi Jacobsen took a step, then grimaced and grabbed Emma's shoulder. "Be my cane for just a minute," he said, "until I know I'm in one piece."

Emma sternly repeated her command to Keppy to "Stay!" She took a gingerly step alongside the rabbi, even as her mind was racing. *How did he survive? He must have been, like, a teenager. I wonder if his parents were killed.*

"Are you so ambitious," Rabbi Jacobsen asked as they hobbled along, "as to be preparing a haftarah passage for the *bimah*?"

"I'm . . . I'm not sure," Emma said. "I'm reading *Ki Tavo*—"

"Ah!" Rabbi Jacobsen chuckled. "I ask about the haftarah and she tells me about the *sidrah* itself! And the book of curses, no less!" He halted to face her. "My father, of blessed memory, when he read the curses in shul, would whisper them. They were an embarrassment to God, he said! Perhaps, young lady, you should instead try Haftarah *Ki Tavo*, from Isaiah." Rabbi Jacobsen's face became luminous as he sang a brief passage in Hebrew, right there on the street. " 'Arise, shine,' " he translated in a joyous voice, " 'for your light has dawned;/The Presence of the Lord has shone upon you!' "

Keppy was whimpering about being left behind. Rabbi Jacobsen took his weight off Emma's shoulder. "I'm all right now," he said. "Go and console your friend."

"She doesn't deserve it," Emma said.

"*Aye, meine tochter,*" the old man said in Yiddish, "every living creature deserves it. You don't need to carry the Torah on your arm"—he patted the spot where Emma had seen his concentration camp tattoo—"to deserve a little consolation." Then he wagged his finger at her. "Remember: Haftarah *Ki Tavo*. Short and sweet."

When Emma returned from her walk with Keppy, she again opened her Torah to the section that Rabbi Jacobsen had called "the book of curses."

> But if you do not obey the Lord your God to observe
> faithfully all His commandments and laws . . .
> Cursed shall you be in the city and cursed shall you be
> in the country.
> Cursed shall be your basket and your kneading bowl.
> Cursed shall be the issue of your womb and the produce
> of your soil, the calving of your herd and the lambing
> of your flock.
> Cursed shall you be in your comings and cursed shall
> you be in your goings."

The curses went on for three pages, threatening the Hebrew people with war, starvation, slavery, even cannibalism, for disobeying God! By comparison, the chapter had less than a page of blessings!

The Mitzvah Machine began to hum. "I know, I know," Emma said, "I have to study the Hebrew, not the English."

The entire monitor filled up with a scrolling list of names:

ABRAHAM	SARAH	LOT	HAGAR
ISHMAEL	ISAAC	NAHOR	MILCAH
BETHUEL	REBEKAH	JACOB	ESAU

LEAH	RACHEL	BILHAH	ZILPAH
REUBEN	SIMEON	LEVI	JUDAH
DAN	NAPHTALI	GAD	ASHER
ISSACHAR	ZEBULUN	DINAH	JOSEPH
BENJAMIN			

They were the biblical characters, starting with Abraham, the first Jew. What in the world was her machine trying to say?

SHIPHRAH	PUAH	YOCHEVED	MIRIAM
MOSES	AARON	ZIPPORAH	GERSHOM
AMRAM	IZHAR	HEBRON	MAHLI
MUSHI			

"Mahli and Mushi! What silly names!"

Next "Mahli" disappeared from the screen, leaving a blank space. The Mitzvah Machine had begun to thin out the list, erasing names in no particular order, even as new ones appeared.

DAVID	ELIJAH	NAOMI	JOSHUA
RUTH	JEREMIAH	ESTHER	EZEKIEL
SAMUEL	MICAH	ZECHARIAH	DEBORAH
DANIEL			

Dave, Eli, Josh, Jerry. . . . Emma giggled. All of these heavy-duty characters from the Torah would have the same nicknames as the kids in her school!

"David" disappeared, and "Ruth," too, right beneath. *Why are they all vanishing?* Emma's thoughts grew dark. Perhaps her machine was displaying a Yom Hashoah lesson that should have been screened over a month ago! Perhaps, then, she would've stayed to hear Rabbi Jacobsen's sermon on Yom

Hashoah and would have found out he was a survivor instead of being startled to learn it on the street today!

"Uch, talk about curses!" she cried to her Mitzvah Machine. *Six million people killed—including a million and a half kids! What could've made God that angry? Even if they all played stupid little pranks like Deborah, or told lies, or even hurt one another. Does that mean God can let six million people die?*

Yes, according to the Torah! "If you do not obey the Lord your God," she read silently again, "to observe faithfully all His commandments and laws . . ." *Slam bam whack whap! What kind of God could do that? Thousands of Davids, thousands of Ruths, slam bam whack whap!*

"Amram," "Esther," "Rachel," "Aaron"—the names were disappearing rapidly from the Mitzvah Machine screen. Soon there'd be hardly any left . . . "Ezekiel," "Naomi," "Daniel," *blip!*

"Wait, bring him back," Emma murmured, uneasy about seeing her best friend's name obliterated. *He's probably on his way to that hospital right now,* she thought. *Maybe I better call him.*

Danny's phone rang and rang without reply. A fearful feeling crept like a spider across Emma's heart. Maybe the Mitzvah Machine was giving a warning: Danny was going to be in an accident on the way to the hospital! Or they'd mix him up with some patient and give him a heart transplant! *Oh, don't be ridiculous,* Emma thought, hanging up the phone, *I'm just going bonkers from thinking about the Holocaust.*

"Deborah" was the next to be obliterated from the Mitzvah Machine screen. "I better go see," Emma decided out loud.

The hospital was near her school on Main Street, a long bike ride or short bus ride away. Emma got permission from her parents to take the bus so that she could study Haftarah *Ki Tavo* en route.

> Arise, shine, for your light has dawned;
> The Presence of the Lord has shone upon you!

The words reminded her of some kind of patriotic song.

> The cry "Violence!"
> Shall no more be heard in your land,
> Nor "Wrack and ruin!"
> Within your borders.

She wondered if people usually made visits to the hospital on Memorial Day. What were people supposed to do on this holiday besides think about soldiers and have a barbecue? What was the history behind it? Emma knew nothing, only that there was no school, and so she was free to be riding the bus in the middle of a Monday! By comparison, Emma realized how much she knew about Jewish holidays by now— the spring calendar was full of them! Purim, Passover, Yom Hashoah, Israeli Independence Day, and Shavuot, each with its own set of rituals, its own Torah readings, its own history and purpose. They were *holy*-days, not just holidays, like Columbus Day or Thanksgiving, which seemed mostly to be about shopping and eating! *Is anyone on this bus "patriotic"?* Emma wondered, looking around for flags, or buttons, or any signs whatsoever of Memorial Day, besides shopping bags.

Yes! The woman seated right next to Emma, an African-American woman, gray-haired and stout, had a black carnation and an American flag pinned to her dress—and she was looking sidelong at Emma's volume of Torah even as Emma was looking sidelong at her corsage.

They exchanged cautious smiles before the woman touched

the flower on her bosom. "For my son," she said in a soft, deep voice with a Southern accent. "He died over there in Vietnam. Twenty years ago."

"Oh, no," Emma cried.

"Yes, he did," the woman said, nodding. "I'm lucky that God blessed me with two more children—they both grown now, got children of their own."

Emma asked the dead son's name.

"Andy," the woman said. "Andrew Malcolm Holmes."

DEBORAH   DANIEL   ANDREW

"Of blessed memory," Emma added shyly.

"Why, thank you!" said Mrs. Holmes with a smile. "Andrew didn't always behave himself, but when he died, I began to realize how much goodness I did lose. I guess we don't count the blessings, none of us do, till we taste the curses."

Emma clutched her Torah against her chest and nodded. "Sometimes," she said quietly, "there seems to be more that's bad. More curses. Or maybe the bad things seem worse than the good things seem good. I don't know. . . ."

"You readin' that Hebrew Bible," Mrs. Holmes observed. "You a Jewish girl?"

Emma nodded again.

"Y'all lost more people from them Nazis than any other family in the world," Mrs. Holmes said. "You know about that, right?"

"There's a kind of Jewish Memorial Day," Emma told her, "called 'Yom Hashoah.' "

"There is? Good!" the woman declared. "Every family and every people got to have their day of mem'ry! I be getting off, now. . . ." The bus was rolling to the curb alongside a cemetery wall.

Emma spoke up as Mrs. Holmes bustled to her feet: "Do you ever feel, like, angry . . . ?"

"About Andy?" Mrs. Holmes said. "Oh, yes, darlin', I was mad about it, I was *burning* up inside. But then there be so much to be mad at: the boy that killed him, the gov'ment that sent him over there, the country that elected the gov'-ment—even the good Lord above. He allowed it to happen, didn't He? So I could spend the rest of my life being *mad,* or else I could spend my time trying to make this world a better place for all of us—including Him." Mrs. Holmes pointed her thumb skywards. "And I made my choice, as God is my witness, I did. And I do believe the Lord is mourning right alongside of me today."

The bus was waiting at the curb, its doors open wide. The driver was sitting very still, listening to Mrs. Holmes without looking at her.

"I'm going to include you in my prayers," Mrs. Holmes said to Emma, "seein' as you included my Andy. We kin, you and me. God bless."

God bless? But God seems to curse more than bless, Emma thought as the bus pulled from the curb. She imagined Mrs. Holmes's brown-skinned arm tattooed in blue, like Rabbi Jacobsen's . . . or black-and-blue, like Deborah Schott's.

Danny was sitting on the hospital steps, scanning the face of every person who entered the glass doors. He did a double take when a face that he peered at turned out to be Emma's. "What are *you* doing here?"

"How does Debby look?" Emma asked.

Danny grimaced. "They won't even let me up to see her! No kids except immediate family, and even then you have to be with a grown-up! I'm just hanging out to see if anybody comes who I know, so at least I can send her a message."

His face brightened. "Hey, maybe *you* can get up to her floor if you say you're her sister, Emma! They haven't seen you at the front desk yet."

Emma shook her head. "I don't want to lie."

"Why?" Danny said sarcastically, glancing at her volume of Torah. "Because God says not to?"

"No. I don't believe in God, if you want to know the truth." Emma sat one step above her friend. "We'd still need an adult to get us in."

"I know, I know." Danny clenched his fist. "Damn!"

"Couldn't you call her on the phone?"

"There *is* no phone—she's in a kids' ward. Damn!"

Emma echoed Danny's curse. Then they smiled at each other and together said: "Damn, damn, damn, damn!"

Danny giggled. "We can have a curse-a-thon!"

"Okay," Emma agreed. She put her arm around his shoulder and together they chanted: "Damn, damn, damn, damn, damn, damn, damn, damn . . ."

"Damn, really!" Danny had tears in his eyes. "What a stupid rule! It's an adult who put Debby in here to begin with! Why should *he* be able to visit, and I'm not? It's not fair!"

"It's not fair," Emma agreed. "The whole world's not fair."

"Damn, damn, damn!" Danny yelled.

"Damn, damn, damn, damn!" Emma joined in, getting louder each time, until the harsh glances of the adults passing in and out of the hospital embarrassed them both into silence.

7

Keppy

What a great dog Keppy is! Emma thought as she threw a stick down the hill and watched the enormous, bushy brown creature bound away after it. *She's so friendly, so loyal. And I love her name! I wonder if having a dog with a Jewish name is enough to make me Jewish, now that I'm an atheist.*

Keppy came back with the stick in her slobbery jaws. "Good girl! Drop it now!"

She mischievously ignored the command and vaulted away when Emma tried to grab the stick. Overflowing with energy, Keppy raced halfway down the hill and back.

"Drop it!" Emma ordered, this time in a stern voice that Keppy obeyed. "Good girl!" Emma squealed again. "You're so happy, aren't you, to have me playing with you instead of studying all the time? Yes!" Keppy jumped up and licked her cheek. Emma laughed and embraced the dog's huge head. "Oh, blessed are *you*, doggy! I bet if you ran the world, there'd be nothing but games to play and sticks to chew!" Then she straightened up and hurled the stick as far as she could, hollering, "Go get it!"

As Keppy scrambled away, Emma looked skywards, beyond the roof of her apartment building, thinking: *I'm an atheist, so there! I don't believe in You! I may not even become a bat mitzvah, so there! Go ahead and do something about it if You exist! But You don't, and I'm glad, because if You did, You'd have to hide Your face in shame.*

"Keppy?" Emma had a sudden attack of anxiety: Where had Keppy gone? She threw her gaze every which way and began calling the dog's name frantically until, to her relief, she saw Keppy all the way across the street, greeting someone very enthusiastically, her tail wagging like mad. Emma wondered if she was supposed to know who he was: a short bald man, oldish-looking, with a trim little beard and a small suitcase.

"Keppy! Keppy, come!"

The man looked up from petting the dog and waved. Emma figured that he was probably some friend of her parents'. In a minute he'd be telling her how much she'd grown since last time he'd seen her and she'd be trying desperately to remember who he was. "Keppy, come!" Emma commanded.

Keppy began to lumber back across the street. "No, wait!" A car was bearing down from the left, too fast along the narrow street. "Stay!" Emma shouted. "Stay!"

Her screams were drowned out by the sound of screeching brakes and a jolting thud. The car swerved and stopped. Emma stumbled headlong down the hill, wailing, "Oh, God, oh, God!"

Keppy burst onto the sidewalk between parked cars. She fell at the very edge of the grassy hill and lay there, panting. Emma slid onto the ground at her side. "Keppy! Help! Somebody! Ma! Momma!"

The little man with the suitcase hurried over and knelt next to the wounded dog. Keppy suddenly became active again, yelping and trying frantically to lick her hind leg, which looked all bent and useless. "She's hurt, she's hurt!" Emma screamed, as the man looked around anxiously for assistance.

The driver of the car, a young man in a T-shirt, was standing near. Traffic was backing up behind his idling car. "The dog ran right out in front of me, I swear!" he said. "I'm sorry, I swear I couldn't do anything!"

"Do something now!" ordered the little man. "Get some help, immediately!"

Emma turned towards her apartment building and again shrieked at the top of her lungs for her mother.

"Is Momma home?" the bearded man asked.

Emma stared at him with tears in her eyes.

"Emma," he said, "I'm your Uncle Izzy. Is Momma home?"

It's a bad dream, she kept telling herself as the minutes ticked away and the grown-ups took over. Her mother, home from work, had been summoned by some neighbors. She was embracing the bald man who had called himself—had he really said it?—Uncle Izzy. The police were arriving. An ASPCA truck was already at the curb, and a veterinarian was looking for the right person to talk to.

"She ran right under my wheels," the driver swore.

It's only a bad dream.

Then Keppy had another fit of pain and fear, yelping and trying to drag herself across the grass to get away from whatever was hurting her—all these strangers! And Emma knew it was real, too real, as she flinched and turned her face away from her beloved dog's agony.

They wouldn't let her near; Keppy might bite, without meaning to, because of the pain, Dr. Cavanaugh said. Emma squatted on the grass at the grown-ups' feet and cooed gently to her dog, who kept blinking and nervously licking her chops, until the pain swelled through her again, and Emma had to look away.

"Izzy!" her mother scolded the little man as the vet examined the injured animal. "Why didn't you let us know you were coming?"

"In Israel," he said with a shrug, "people drop in unexpectedly. It's the way of life. I thought to give you a little taste of the Holy Land, to surprise you for Shavuot, tonight. Only to be met by this . . . ach!"

"The Mitzvah Machine!" Emma suddenly cried. "Uncle Izzy!"

"Darling girl!"

"The Mitzvah Machine! Maybe it can do something!"

"Oh, Emma, what can a computer do now?" said her mother.

"You don't know!" Emma replied, waving her off. "I haven't told hardly anybody! It's magical! It *is*! Uncle Izzy . . ."

Another yelp from Keppy silenced them all.

"Please," Emma sobbed, "the machine keeps making things happen!"

"What kinds of things?" he asked.

"Miracles!" she said. "The very first time I ever plugged it in, it made a blackout in the whole building, and then—"

" 'Tzedakah,' it said, hm?"

"Yes!" Emma cried.

"It was your birthday," Uncle Izzy explained, patting her head. "I programmed the machine to say 'Tzedakah' to remind you that it's a mitzvah to give tzedakah on such occasions as birthdays."

"But as soon as I said it," she argued, "the lights went out!"

"A coincidence," he insisted.

"And when I said it again—"

Her mother shushed her. Dr. Cavanaugh was ready to speak to them.

Keppy had a shattered hind leg and had to be x-rayed,

the vet reported. Perhaps there were internal injuries to Keppy's organs as well. "I won't know until some tests are run." She looked directly at Emma. "I've got to bring your dog to the shelter. She'll stay with us overnight. The next twenty-four hours are very, very important. What's her name?"

"Keppy."

"Can you help us get Keppy on the stretcher? I think it's all right if you approach her now. Just try to keep her calm."

Emma knelt beside her Enormous Dog. Keppy's tail twitched once, in greeting. "Shh." Emma lowered her face to Keppy's floppy ear. "Good girl, Keppy. You're such a good girl. I love you, Keppy." As Emma whispered and rubbed her dog's muzzle, Dr. Cavanaugh and the driver of the ASPCA animal ambulance managed to slip a stretcher under Keppy.

As they lifted her, the dog yelped with pain and then lay very, very still. The truck looked like an oversized ice cream truck, with a dozen silver-handled compartments. Keppy was slid into the largest one. The driver latched the door shut.

Sharon embraced Emma, and the girl began to cry unconsolably.

"She'll be all right," Uncle Izzy said from behind them. "Emma, Keppy's going to be all right. Didn't your Uncle Izzy predict how big your puppy would grow? I'm telling you now, and you must believe me: Keppy's going to be fine."

Emma shook her head and lifted her teary face to the sky. "Why is God so mean?" she sobbed.

"Come, baby," Sharon said. She gathered Emma into her arms and carried her like a toddler towards their building.

"Tell me more about these 'miracles' that the Mitzvah Machine performs," Uncle Izzy said as he visited his tearful niece in her room.

"I don't want to talk about it." Emma was propped up

against pillows on her bed, staring out the window at gathering darkness.

Izzy sat at the foot of her bed. "Do you want to pray, instead, for Keppy?"

"No!" Emma rose up on her knees. "Uncle Izzy, how can you believe in God! What kind of God would let my dog get hurt?"

Izzy sighed: "Oy! What kind of God? A busy God. Tonight, after all, our God is preparing for *Zeman Mattan Toratenu*— the time of the giving of our Torah. Tonight is Shavuot! God is cooking a meal for six hundred thousand visitors! Tonight we all stand at Mount Sinai, without a Mitzvah Machine, to receive the Torah directly."

Emma shook her head miserably. "I don't believe it! So the Bible says we stood at Sinai and saw a bunch of lightning! So what? We also stood inside gas chambers! I learned about that in Hebrew school, too! Our own rabbi's a survivor! I saw the numbers on his arm! What kind of God could let *that* happen?"

"What kind of God?" Izzy stroked his beard and sighed again. "A sad God. A grieving God. But don't you think the more important question to ask is what kind of people could let it happen? Hm? What kind of world could let the Holocaust happen? Don't you see, Emma?" He slid closer to her on the bed. "God is all of us. The whole human race. My mother used to say, whenever I did a mitzvah,"—Izzy pretended to have a thick Yiddish accent—" 'De whole voild should see dis t'ing you do, Isadore.' And I would say, 'Momma, how can the whole world see anything? Do you realize how big the world is, how many people there are?' And Momma would say, *'Mit Gott fun Himmel'*—with God in heaven—'anything is possible.' Oy, Momma!" Izzy exclaimed, enjoying his memory. "But what did she mean, Emma?"

Emma pulled a pillow to her chest.

"Did she really think that the whole world was going to know that her little Isadore had given a little tzedakah?" Izzy continued. "Of course not. What Momma was saying was that *if* the whole world could share the mitzvah, *if* at a kind moment you could speak to the whole world, *if* at such a loving moment you could look into everyone's eyes at once . . ."

Emma smiled at the thought of her uncle as a little boy—she imagined him still, with his beard and bald head—being watched by the entire world, every single person pausing. Then the smile vanished from Emma's face as she remembered: "It seemed like slow motion when that car hit Keppy. Everything stopped. Everything."

"God came near," Izzy said in a hushed tone. "God came near, and it felt as if the whole world were watching. Hm? Because Keppy was hurt, and your heart was full of pain. Perhaps that's when God comes closest—when you want to speak to the whole world, and cannot . . . you want to cry to the whole world, and cannot. That's when you look *up*. You speak, *up*." Uncle Izzy gestured towards the ceiling with a grand sweep of his arms. Then he sang:

"*Shema . . . Yisrael . . . Adonai . . . Elohenu . . . Adonai . . . Echad!*"

The Mitzvah Machine began to hum.

TIKKUN LEIL SHAVUOT

THIS NIGHT, IT IS CUSTOMARY TO STAY AWAKE ALL NIGHT, STUDYING TORAH. TRADITIONALLY, WE STUDY A SMALL SECTION FROM EVERY BOOK OF THE BIBLE AND EVERY SECTION OF TALMUD.

"Ah! This is the Shavuot lesson I prepared for you," Uncle Izzy recalled.

"I'm such an idiot!" Emma said bitterly. "I actually thought the Mitzvah Machine was, like, magical!"

"Learning Torah *is* magical," he insisted, as the machine hummed and printed:

READ IN TORAH: GENESIS 18:22-33

"Abraham's argument with God about destroying the sinful city of Sodom," Uncle Izzy said. "He makes God promise that if there are even ten good people in the city, the whole place will be spared. Arguing with God . . ."—Uncle Izzy took his niece's chin into his hands and looked into her eyes— "this, too, is Torah."

READ IN TORAH: EXODUS 20:1-14

"The Ten Commandments," Uncle Izzy said. "The essentials of what enables us all to live together. Living together . . ."— he took Emma by the chin again—"this, too, is Torah."

READ IN TORAH: LEVITICUS 19:9

" 'When you reap the harvest of your land,' " Uncle Izzy recited from memory, " 'you shall not reap all the way to the edges of your field, or gather the gleanings of your harvest. . . . You shall leave them for the poor and the stranger. . . .' " Emma smiled this time as her uncle lifted her face by the chin. "Giving to those who need—this, too, is Torah."

"Emma?" Bruce and Sharon were standing in the doorway of her room. "I've just been on the phone with the ASPCA," her father reported. "So far, so good. Keppy's hind leg is broken, and the hip has a fracture."

"Oh, God!" Emma cried, feeling her dog's pain.

"But they've found no internal injuries," Bruce continued. "That's good news, honey! If Keppy can survive the shock, I think she may pull through."

"Of course she will!" Uncle Izzy declared.

"Can't we go see her?" pleaded Emma.

Sharon knelt at her bedside. "The building is closed for the night, darling. Even their switchboard is shutting down now. We won't be able to find out anything more until morning."

"I won't be able to sleep all night," Emma replied sadly.

"Then we'll stay up all night, for Shavuot!" Izzy announced.

"We will not!" said Emma's father.

"Ah!" Izzy cried, and pointed towards the window. "Look!"

Fireflies were popping everywhere at once in the darkness. One of them was on the pane, glowing mysteriously. "The Jewish mystical books," said Izzy excitedly, "say that when God created the world, God, who was everywhere, had to withdraw to make space. God had to shrink a little, to make room for the world! And little sparks of light that God left behind were everywhere. Like these . . ."

The greenish color of the fireflies' lights reminded Emma of the Mitzvah Machine's hue. She glanced over to see what the monitor was saying now. Her dad smiled at her and made a circling gesture with his finger at his temple. *Uncle Izzy,* he was saying, *is as crazy as ever.*

"It is our job," Izzy went on, with mounting excitement, "to collect these holy sparks and repair all of creation!"

"Uncle Iz," Bruce said, "they're just fireflies."

Izzy turned to him with a wild shake of his head. "*Just* fireflies? And this . . . ?" He put his arm around Emma.

"This is *just* your daughter? And Keppy is *just* a dog? And this world . . . this world is *just* a world, so we might as well all go to sleep?"

"Take it easy," Bruce said sheepishly.

"Come!" Uncle Izzy held his hand out to Emma. "Let's go out to collect some holy sparks!"

"I'll give you a couple of glass jars," Sharon volunteered. "You can punch holes in the tops."

Emma remained on her bed. "I don't believe in this stuff anymore, Uncle Izzy," she insisted.

"Never mind believing!" Izzy waved his hand impatiently. "In Judaism, we do the mitzvah first—*then* we believe. That way, even if we *never* believe, the mitzvah gets done. Come now. I'm a visitor from Jerusalem. Show me your neighborhood. If God is walking around, you'll introduce us. If not— we'll *just* see the fireflies!"

Uncle Izzy plucked a few leaves from an oak tree that stood alongside the spot where Keppy had greeted him so happily moments before the accident. It was traditional at Shavuot, he explained to Emma, to decorate the home and the synagogue with branches, green plants, flowers. The holiday had many meanings, he said, including that of a harvest festival.

That spot was the first of many that reminded Emma of Keppy, of their jaunts around the neighborhood. Watching Izzy chasing fireflies with Keppy's kind of clumsy, playful energy, Emma could not stop worrying about her dog. What could Keppy be thinking, lying in some cage in a hospital, alone and suffering? Emma would gladly have spent the night in a cage to be with her. *Keppy, good girl,* she kept thinking, beaming her thoughts skywards as she wondered in which direction, north, south, east, or west, the animal hospital stood.

Wherever you are, Keppy, go to sleep now. I'll see you tomorrow! We haven't left you, my love! Go to sleep, Keppy.

"You're still thinking," Izzy remarked, observing her face, "about God and the evil of this world, hm?"

Emma shook her head. "I'm thinking about Keppy."

"Of course."

"Uncle Izzy, do you believe in mental telepathy?"

"Projecting your thoughts so others can hear them?"

"Yes. I wish I could do that with Keppy right now."

"Ah! With God as the switchboard operator." Izzy pretended to be dialing a telephone. "Hello, Keppy?" Then he began to speak in Hebrew.

"What are you saying?" Emma asked.

" 'May the Lord bless you and keep you,' " he translated. " 'May the Lord's face shine upon you and be gracious unto you. May the Lord's face lift up towards you and grant you peace.' It's the Priestly Benediction," he explained. "A very special prayer, which we offer tonight for Keppy—via mental telepathy! Come now! Show me all of Keppy's favorite spots. At each one we will catch a firefly, a holy spark to restore her health."

But the night was deepening and the fireflies were starting to vanish. Emma was exhausted from the tension of the day. She barely managed to reach the top of the hill where the grass was bald. Izzy cheered as he trapped a firefly in his jar. "How many do we have now?" Two in his jar, five in Emma's. "Seven! A holy number. God created the world in six days, and on the seventh God rested."

"I want to rest, too," said Emma. "Can we go home?"

Back in the apartment, Izzy immediately announced his intention to bake bread, two loaves of challah, to represent the two tablets that Moses carried down from Mount Sinai. Sharon showed him around the kitchen and then decided to help, despite the fact that it was ten o'clock at night and the bread baking would take at least four hours.

Emma carried the fireflies back into her room. The Mitzvah Machine had something new on its screen:

ARISE, SHINE, FOR YOUR LIGHT
HAS DAWNED;
THE PRESENCE OF THE LORD HAS
SHONE UPON YOU!

Emma recognized it at once: the opening lines of Haftarah *Ki Tavo,* the section from the Book of Isaiah, which she had been studying for her bat mitzvah. Rabbi Jacobsen had sung and translated these very lines to her, right there on the street, after Keppy had knocked him down.

—*Shh, don't kick.*

—*She deserves it! You bad dog, Keppy! You stay put now!*

I kicked her right in the spot where her bones are now broken, Emma thought ruefully. *How could I? How could I?*

She began to sob, with her face in her pillow so that none of the grown-ups would hear. She wanted to be alone with her grief, her guilt, her memories, in her godless world. She wanted to be like Keppy in her cage: alone, without another soul to comfort her. But the Mitzvah Machine was humming again. "Be quiet!" she whispered hoarsely. "Can't you just leave me alone?"

RAISE YOUR EYES AND LOOK ABOUT:
THEY HAVE ALL GATHERED AND COME TO YOU.
YOUR SONS SHALL BE BROUGHT FROM AFAR,
YOUR DAUGHTERS LIKE BABES ON SHOULDERS.

More of Haftarah *Ki Tavo!* "I don't want to study now!" Emma insisted, and then reminded herself: *It's just a machine.*

It can't hear you and it's not going to obey! Everything that happened, it's all just coincidence. There's no magic in this world, Emma Ansky-Levine! No magic, no miracles!

She draped her blanket over the monitor to block out its light. Now the only light in her room came from the jars of fireflies. Still, she could not be alone, for she could hear the pots and pans rattling in the kitchen. She could see the lights in the windows of all the apartments in the building on the other side of the hill. She could imagine herself among six hundred thousand people at the foot of a mountain, each of them waiting for something absolutely incredible to happen. Tonight, Jewish people all over the world were awake with her: baking, decorating, studying, discussing . . . or maybe just sitting quietly, petting their cats or their dogs and thinking about night and day, about good and evil, about life and death, about love and loneliness . . .

Oh, God, Emma prayed at last, with her forehead against the windowpane, *everyone's got something different to say about you! I don't understand and I don't even know if you're there, but if you are, please, tonight, just take care of my dog. Even if you're busy. Please.*

Then she heard a fluttering sound: the fireflies. She opened one of her window screens, screwed off the tops of the jars, and let the insects fly off with their green lights trailing. Maybe one of them would carry its light to Keppy, fly into the animal hospital and beep out a Morse Code message . . .

ARISE, SHINE, FOR YOUR LIGHT
HAS DAWNED . . .

Emma climbed onto her bed and propped herself in the darkness against the pillows. *Good girl, Keppy . . . good girl, sweet girl . . . You'll be okay, honey. Everything's okay. . . . "Arise, shine, for your light has dawned;/The Presence of the Lord has shone upon you!/Arise, shine! . . ."*

The next thing Emma knew the telephone was ringing and there was daylight at the window. It was morning, and she was still in yesterday's clothes! Emma jumped out of bed and picked up the receiver. Her mom was already on with Dr. Cavanaugh:

". . . doing very well—much better than we expected. She'll need to be in a cast, and we don't know yet how the hip will mend, but the worst dangers of shock are past and there are no internal injuries, which is really quite a miracle given the kind of accident . . ."

"Emma?" Sharon said. "Emma, are you on the phone? Did you hear, honey? Keppy's going to be okay!"

Emma was weeping for joy.

"I think she's a little overwhelmed," Sharon told the doctor.

"Perfectly understandable," Dr. Cavanaugh said.

"Arise and shine!" Uncle Izzy called through Emma's door. "Emma! I have fresh challah for you."

Emma raced to the door with tears dripping down her nose. "Uncle Izzy, Keppy's okay! She's okay!" She threw open the door. Izzy was standing there, bedraggled and exhausted.

"It's a miracle!" Emma sniffled. "Keppy's okay! She's not going to die! Oh, thank God!"

"Thank who?" Izzy kidded as she threw her arms around him.

8

The Important Thing

Dear Family and Friends:
My mom, Sharon Ansky,
and my dad, Bruce Levine,
and I,
Emma Ansky-Levine,
have the pleasure of inviting you
to my bat mitzvah
on Saturday morning,
September 13, 10 A.M.
at Temple Beth Shalom,
15 Willow Street.
There'll be a party afterwards,
with lots of good things to eat and drink,
and with lots of dancing,
starting at 3:00 P.M.,
in the community room of our building,
41 Hillcrest Avenue.
Please RSVP by phone or mail
by August 21,
and when you do,
please tell me your answer to this question:
What, to you, is the most important thing about Judaism?
(You don't have to be Jewish to answer!)

Every morning in August, Emma would wait with her limping dog by the mailboxes, eager for Sandra, the mail carrier, to finish stuffing the boxes so that Emma

103

could read the replies to her invitation. Some people wrote long letters—such as Uncle Ed, Bruce's older brother, who owned a bookstore in Vermont:

"Dear Emma, I don't think your father or I really ever thought very much about the question you ask. Except for Uncle Izzy, our whole family was never very religiously identified. Our parents thought of that stuff as fairly backward, and we celebrated our bar mitzvahs only for the sake of our grandparents. I guess for me, given the work I do, the most important thing about Judaism is the love for books. . . ."

Other people's replies were very short—such as Mrs. G's:

"Most important? *Rachmones:* compassion. The Jewish heart, may it never stop beating."

A couple of others made Emma think *I have so much to learn about*—such as the note from Uncle Izzy himself, who was traveling around the country, visiting other relatives:

"The most important thing about Judaism is the mitzvah, and the highest mitzvah, in my humble opinion, is aliyah to Israel. See you in shul, Emma."

One of the responses made her cry. She found it not in her mailbox, but on her pillow on the morning of August 21:

"The most important thing about Judaism, to us, is the excitement that we see in your eyes. We're so proud of you we could burst. Love, Mom & Dad."

I'm so proud of you, too, Emma thought as she stood with Bruce and Sharon on the *bimah* and heard them recite, with tears in their eyes, the parental blessing in Hebrew that they had worked hard to master: "*Baruch shepetarani me'ansho shelazeh*—Blessed is the One who has freed me from responsibility for this child's conduct."

The three of them embraced. "I love you," Emma whispered,

giving an extra squeeze. Her parents then returned to their seats, leaving Emma standing alone to deliver her *devar Torah*.

"I'm so relieved to be finished with the Hebrew!" she began.

"It was wonderful!" someone called out.

"Thank you! Listen, just because my parents are now finished being responsible for me, can that just mean now you're *all* responsible for me? Okay?"

Then she began her speech in earnest, taking a deep breath and thinking about her Mitzvah Machine's response to her invitation. It had appeared on the screen on the morning of the RSVP date, August 21:

MICAH 6:8
''IT HAS BEEN TOLD TO YOU, O MAN,
WHAT IS GOOD,
AND WHAT THE LORD REQUIRES OF YOU:
ONLY TO DO JUSTICE
AND TO LOVE GOODNESS,
AND TO WALK HUMBLY WITH YOUR GOD.''

MAZEL TOV, EMMA!

"An important teacher of mine," Emma said, looking down from the *bimah* at all the friendly faces, "answered my invitation by quoting to me from the prophet Micah. Micah reduces all six hundred and thirteen of Judaism's commandments to just three: we should do justice, love goodness, and walk humbly with our God. Another teacher of mine . . ."—she looked sidelong at Rabbi Jacobsen, seated at the eastern wall— "wrote me a note about Hillel, the greatest scholar of the days of the Temple. Hillel was asked to summarize Judaism while he stood on one foot. And he did it! He said, 'Whatever's hateful to you, don't do to your neighbor. That's the whole Torah—the rest is commentary.' And then he told the guy who was asking to go and study!

"A lot of you people wrote some interesting things, too," Emma said, holding up a long sheet of paper. "Like my friend Danny: 'The most important thing about Judaism is the food, especially chopped liver!' " The sanctuary rippled with laughter. Danny sat wedged between his parents with a proud grin on his face.

Emma continued: "And my cousin Jessica: 'The most important thing is knowing Jewish history, especially the long history of struggling for justice.' And my friend Reba Klein . . ." Reba looked neat, if a little dorky, in a pink blouse with a big bow and black velvet slacks. She bowed her head shyly as Emma read: " 'What counts about Judaism is recognizing the holiness of our world—of everything in it.'

"Then there's Mrs. Trible, my neighbor: 'What counts is for Jewish people to be safe from harm, to have dignity, and to be appreciated for all that they've given to the world.' " Mrs. Trible, in her wheelchair, was heard to say "Amen" from her place of honor along the eastern wall.

"Among the things that Jews gave to the world," Emma continued, "was Sigmund Freud, who was the founder of psychoanalysis. He made up theories about why people do the things they do, especially the crazy things! Freud said something really interesting about Judaism: that being Jewish gave him the freedom to be a pioneer, a freethinker, a nonconformist. That's also what my mother's friend from college, Carol Kirsch, said: 'The important thing is the freedom to be different.' Carol likes Sigmund Freud, you see—she's a therapist."

Everyone was laughing, nodding, beaming at Emma. She continued to read from the list of responses to the question on her invitation and sprinkled in quotes from famous Jewish people—Albert Einstein, Henrietta Szold, Martin Buber, Emma Lazarus, the Baal Shem Tov. Some spoke about Zionism and Israel as most important; others about the Holocaust and Jewish survival; others about Shabbat, about God, about the Torah, about the covenant, about Jewish peoplehood. . . .

"You see," Emma summed up, waving the paper again, "there are more opinions about Judaism than there are people in this room! And I've had a hard time with that. I think kids like to have answers. We'd like to know that *somebody* knows what's going on! That's why we get frustrated, for instance, when our parents *answer* a question by *asking* a question—like, you say, 'What should I be when I grow up?' and they say, 'What would you *like* to be when you grow up?'

"But today's my bat mitzvah," Emma went on, "which means I'm supposed to be on my way to being grown-up. And I think part of being a grown-up is understanding that there are no easy answers, not in life, and not in Judaism, either. It's like the story that Mrs. G tells about two guys who are having an argument and they bring their argument to the rabbi to settle it. And the rabbi listens to the first guy and says, 'Hm, it sounds like you're right.' And the rabbi listens to the second guy and says, 'Hm, it sounds like you're right.' So someone else in the synagogue says, 'Wait a minute, rabbi. These two are contradicting each other, so how can you say that they're both right?' And the rabbi says, 'Hm, it sounds like *you're* also right!' "

Emma waited for the laughter to subside. "The only thing I don't like about the story is that it's all guys. So from now on I'm making it a woman rabbi."

"Named 'Emma,' we hope!" cried Mrs. G from the front row of benches.

Emma blew her a kiss and continued: "I've learned, over this past year, not so much to look for answers as to look for the right kinds of questions. Questions like: How does what I'm doing affect other people? How would I act, right now, if I knew that God was watching? Being Jewish means you have a lot of places where you can ask these questions. You can ask your teacher, your rabbi, the Torah, even God!— and you can also learn how to ask yourself.

"Judaism's a kind of discussion, in other words—a discussion about what's important in life. That's why, whenever someone comes along who wants to squelch the discussion— for instance, a dictator, or a religious leader who wants people to think he's got all the answers—that's when anti-Semitism starts to spread, and Jews get picked on.

"Now, if Judaism's a discussion, it's important for us to realize that there are all kinds of Jews who need a turn to speak. Maybe that's what the haftarah means . . ." Emma again referred to her sheet of paper: " 'Raise your eyes and look about:/They have all gathered and come to you.' " She looked up at her audience and smiled. " 'They have all gathered and come to you.' Jews who are atheists, and Jews who think they can't tie their shoes without God watching. Jews who are survivors of the Holocaust, and Jews who are survivors of other kinds of violence—and Jews who are violent themselves, unfortunately.

" 'They have all gathered and come to you,' " Emma repeated. "Jews who are white and Jews who are black and Jews who are every shade in between. Jews who are geniuses and Jews who are mentally retarded, Jews who are Olympic athletes and Jews in wheelchairs. There are Jews who get married and Jews who stay single, and there are Jews who wish they could get married to the person they love but can't because they're gay. There are Jews who are rich and Jews who are homeless. There are Jews who believe in obeying God—whatever that means—and there are Jews who believe in arguing with God—whatever *that* means!

"I think the important thing," Emma concluded, "is that there are Jews, period. The important thing is that the discussion goes on. Which means that *all* Jews should count. Any one of them might be the next Queen Esther. Any one of them might be the prophet Elijah. Any one of them might be among the six hundred thousand Jews at Mount Sinai at Shavuot.

"Every one of them's a person, anyway. And Judaism says, every person is made in God's image. That means, when we look in each other's eyes, we're seeing God; when we mistreat each other, we're mistreating God; when we help each other, we're helping God. I guess our relationships are pretty awesome, if you think about them that way—if you 'raise your eyes and look about,' and learn to see with the heart.

"That's really all I want to say. I hope I didn't sound too preachy. I also want to say, 'Thanks a lot.' You've all been my teachers. So, thanks a lot."

"Thank *you,* Emma," said old Rabbi Jacobsen as he approached the *bimah* once again.

Emma was being mobbed by everyone with cries of *"Yasher koach!"* and *"Mazel tov!"* when she glimpsed Uncle Izzy's white beard and bald head at the outer perimeter of the crowd. Her heart filled with tender feelings, and she worked her way through the crush of bodies saying "Excuse me, excuse me" to all her well-wishers.

He had his little suitcase with him! "Uncle Izzy, aren't you coming to my party?"

"We'll make our own party," he said. "I've got to get my house ready for your visit."

"What visit? What do you mean?"

Uncle Izzy handed her an envelope and told her to open it. Inside, Emma found a round-trip airplane ticket to Ben-

Gurion Airport in Israel! She shrieked and threw her arms around Uncle Izzy as he murmured, "We'll light the menorah together, hm?"

"Oh, Uncle Izzy," she said as they embraced, "you're really the one who started the whole discussion!"

"Remember the words of Hillel, now," he instructed her. " 'Go study!' "

"No problem," Emma boasted, "as long as I have the Mitzvah Machine!"

Izzy pursed his lips and was about to reply when Bill and Vanessa Trible grabbed Emma to congratulate her on her wonderful performance. Vanessa, Emma noticed, was wearing a gorgeous, hand-painted purple scarf. *I wonder if she'll give me something like that for a present. . . .*

When she looked back to say a final farewell to her uncle, Izzy had disappeared. Emma's mom stood in his place. "Emma," she said, "we've got a party to prepare for," and then she mouthed the words "Let's go."

Something about their apartment door was different, so different that Emma hesitated before putting her key in the lock. The old gouge on the doorjamb, by which she had always distinguished her apartment, even when she was little and couldn't yet read the "10-E" beneath the peephole, was now covered by a wooden ornament. It was shaped like the tablets of the Ten Commandments, with an inlaid Hebrew letter, *shin,* carved from a lighter-colored wood. Emma recognized it as a mezuzah—Danny's family had one on their door, made of brass. She knew it would contain, inside, a parchment with the *Shema*—"Hear, O Israel! . . ."—inscribed on it.

"Who put up the mezuzah?" she asked her parents, who were impatient to get inside.

Neither of them could answer. "Maybe it's a gift from

Uncle Izzy," Sharon said, and began calling his name as she entered the apartment.

"Mom?" Emma said. "Didn't Uncle Izzy say goodbye to you?"

Sharon halted in the foyer. "Goodbye? What do you mean?"

"He said he was going back to Israel," Emma said. "And he gave me this." She showed her parents the envelope with the airplane ticket.

"If that isn't like Uncle Izzy!" Bruce said, half-amused and half-annoyed. "Always dramatic! Always appearing from nowhere and disappearing to the same place! Once, when I was a kid, we had this Passover seder. I don't know how he did it, but one second Izzy's at the table with us, and when we open the door for Elijah, he's standing outside! I think he must have used the fire escape."

"Can I still go to Israel for Chanukah?" Emma asked fretfully.

"Oh, of course," Sharon said. "He spoke to us in advance about *that*! I'm just *so* disappointed he won't be at our party!" Sharon glanced at the mezuzah again. "It's a lovely thing," she murmured, touching the *shin*.

Keppy came limping over to greet the family. Emma scratched the dog's great big head. "C'mon, let's go check the Mitzvah Machine for messages."

As she walked with Keppy into her room, Emma was jolted by the same feeling she'd had at the door to the apartment. Something was different—her desk looked naked. "Where's the Mitzvah Machine?" she cried. "Dad! Mom!"

Bruce rushed in. "How can it be?" he said, staring at the blank area on her desk. "The front door was locked, wasn't it?"

"Yes! You saw me use my key!"

Bruce checked the windows. "No one but Superman could

come ten stories up. I don't know, Emma . . ." He turned to face her. "Maybe Uncle Izzy has been up to his old tricks."

"He was only carrying his little suitcase," Emma insisted. "He couldn't possibly have fit the Mitzvah Machine in there!"

"Let me see if anything else in the house is missing. Sharon? Sharon!"

"Keppy," Emma said as her father walked out, "where's the Mitzvah Machine?"

Keppy wagged her tail and shifted her gaze from Emma's face to the desk. Emma's open volume of Torah was lying there, alongside where Uncle Izzy's invention used to be. Emma looked down at the page, expecting to see the haftarah for *Ki Tavo.*

The book was open to Deuteronomy 6:4–9 instead: the *Shema.* Emma could almost hear the Mitzvah Machine humming as she read:

> Hear, O Israel! The Lord is our God, the Lord is one.
> You shall love the Lord your God with all your heart
> and with all your soul and with all your might. Take to
> heart these instructions with which I charge you this day.
> Impress them upon your children. Recite them when you
> stay at home and when you are away, when you lie down
> and when you get up. Bind them as a sign on your hand
> and let them serve as a symbol on your forehead; inscribe
> them on the doorposts of your house . . .

"The doorposts?" Emma wondered.

Bruce ducked his head into the room. "There's nothing else missing, honey. Uncle Izzy must be designing a new, improved model for you."

Emma nodded thoughtfully. "You may be right, Dad." Then she looked Keppy in the eye. "Keppy, find the Mitzvah Machine. Go fetch!"

Keppy limped from the room, claws clicking against the parquet floor. She led Emma and her father back to the threshold of the apartment, where Sharon was still staring at the mezuzah. "It's such an exquisite piece of work!" Sharon explained, embarrassed to be lingering over it so long.

"Keppy," Emma whispered in her dog's ear, "is *that* it?"

Keppy licked Emma's nose and nuzzled her neck.

"I think Keppy may need to go out," her mother observed.

"Nah," Emma said, and giggled. "She just likes the mezuzah."

"Hey, let's snap out of it, gang!" Bruce declared. "We've got a party to organize!"

"Oh, right!" Emma hollered, leading the charge towards the kitchen. "The important thing: chopped liver!"